As The World Dies
Untold Tales
Volume Two

Rhiannon Frater

As the World Dies: Untold Tales V.2
By Rhiannon Frater

Original Copyright 2012 by Rhiannon Frater
All Rights Reserved.

Edited by Felicia A. Sullivan
Interior formatting by Kody Boye
Cover Artwork and Layout by Philip Rogers

ISBN-13:9781470081362
ISBN-10:1470081369

http://rhiannonfrater.com/
http://astheworlddies.com/

This book is a work of fiction. People, places, events and situation are the product of the author's imagination. Any resemblance to actual persons, living, dead or undead, or historical events, is purely coincidental.

Author's Note:

The three stories you are about to read are a perfect segue into SIEGE, the last book in the AS THE WORLD DIES zombie trilogy. Every character in the stories plays a role in SIEGE in some capacity. In some cases, the journey started in these short stories come full circle in SIEGE.

The stories in UNTOLD TALES VOLUME 2 provide an intriguing backdrop to the events in the third book.

I hope you enjoy all three stories and the small glimpses you will get into the lives of the people who inhabit the AS THE WORLD DIES universe.

Eternally,
Rhiannon Frater
February 21, 2012

Also by Rhiannon Frater

As the World Dies Series
The First Days
Fighting to Survive
Siege (Spring 2012 from Tor)
Untold Tales, V1.

Pretty When She... Series
Pretty When She Dies: A Vampire Novel

Vampire Bride Series
The Tale of the Vampire Bride
The Vengeance of the Vampire Bride

The Living Dead Boy and the Zombie Hunters

Short Story Collections
Blood and Love and Other Vampire Tales
Cthulu's Daughter and Other Tales of Horror

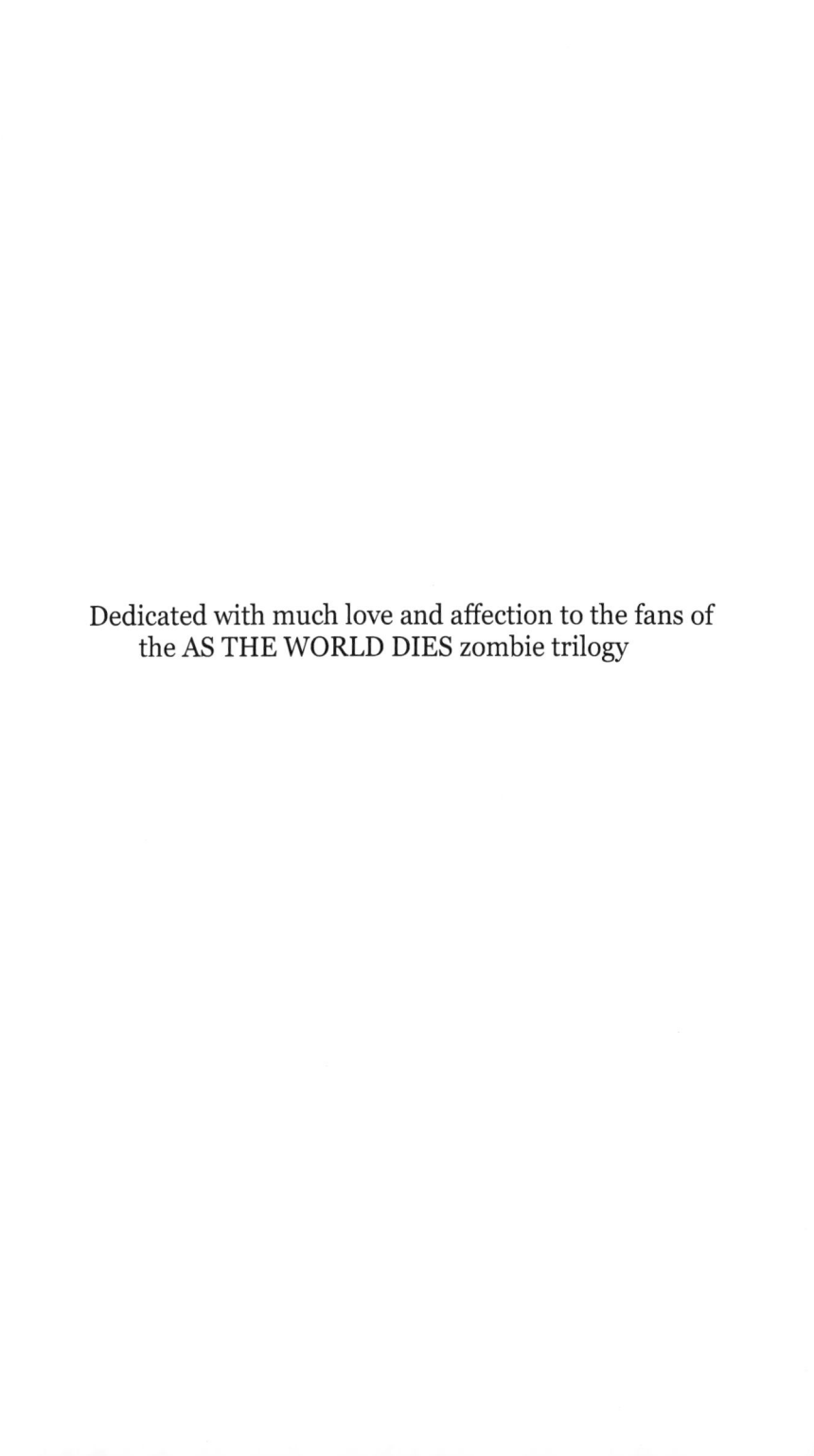

Dedicated with much love and affection to the fans of
the AS THE WORLD DIES zombie trilogy

Table of Contents

Revelation 1

A Terrible Moment 15

Friendship in the Time of Zombies 31

Katarina's Story

Katarina has been in the series since THE FIRST DAYS. Though she is not a major character, she has always garnered fan love. I have had many emails asking me to write an untold tale about the plain redhead. Nerit's protégée has always had a vital role in the fort, but her past was shrouded in mystery.

The online serial briefly touched on her *first day* story, but it was removed from the Tor edition of SIEGE. As I was working on the revision, I realized her back story didn't fit smoothly in the narrative and felt tacked on. I was sad to remove it, but suddenly realized it would make a great untold tale.

I'm very pleased to present Katarina's *first day* story fully realized and expanded upon for your reading pleasure.

Revelation

    The hot dinner plate was burning her hand, her feet were aching in her sneakers, and the throbbing pain nestled between her shoulder blades seemed to be settling in for the long haul. Katarina wanted nothing more than to take a few Advil, soak her feet, and lay on the sofa at home with an ice pack. Sadly, the breakfast shift wasn't over for another hour in the small diner decorated in Coke Cola memorabilia.
    Maneuvering around crowded tables in the cafe, she aimed for the booth in the far corner. A knot of dread filled her chest as she drew closer. She dreaded dealing with the man seated there.
    Randall was a regular customer in the cafe. A long haul trucker, his route took him straight through Ashley Oaks every few weeks. He always stopped to grab coffee and a hot plate of food. His shorn head and scruffy beard, coupled with his

usual plaid shirt and heavy boots, always made Katarina think of a lumberjack. Though he always left her very good tips, she didn't like him in the least. His shrewd eyes were a little too keen on her. She was nothing to look at with her unruly red hair, weak chin, freckles, and pale eyes, but he seemed to relish directing his unwanted attentions on her. It had taken her a long time to figure out that what she didn't like about his blatant flirting was that he wasn't doing it because he was attracted to her, but because he could see she didn't like it. Her discomfort was his enjoyment.

"Oh, good enough to eat," he said as she slid the plate down in front of him. As usual, he wasn't looking at the food, but at her. "Delicious and pink, tasty and savory. And just a little salty, I guess?"

"The ham is fresh. Just had it delivered yesterday," she answered quickly, setting down his silverware and a few extra napkins.

"I like things fresh," he said, grinning, his eyes on her neck. He had once traced the edge of her collarbone with his fingertips. She had taken a very hot shower to remove the memory of his thick, dry fingers.

Even though her uniform was very modest, pale blue with a white apron, skirt to her knees, her collar just below her collarbone, he always made her feel as though she was flashing an intimate part of her body.

"I'll get you more coffee," Katarina said, and made a hasty escape.

Though flustered, she remembered to check on her other tables, smiling in spite of her exhaustion and her discomfort. She could feel Randall's eyes watching her from across the room.

The diner was open twenty-four hours, catering mostly to the truckers passing through the area. Though they were not on an interstate, trucks cut through the area trying to shave off time. The old highway at the edge of Ashley Oaks was usually busy with only locals and truck drivers. Tourists never made it out this way, though city hall was working hard to make the town a new tourist trap like Fredericksburg or Marfa, Texas. The reconstruction downtown was impressive so far with the hotel being restored, but Katarina thought it was all a pipe dream. Did anyone really care that, back in the golden age of Hollywood, movie stars had vacationed in Ashley Oaks?

"Hey, boys," Katarina said, checking on a table packed with construction workers. Most of them were new to the area, but she had known Juan since they were in elementary school together. Travis was new, but she knew him because of the massive crush one of the other waitresses had on him. "How's the food?"

"Great. Almost as good as my mom's," Juan answered in his thick West Texas drawl. He was a cute one with green eyes and curly dark hair. He was descended from a long line of cowboys and Katarina liked his gentlemanly manner.

"I'll let the cook know," Katarina said with a grin.

"Brenda's not working this morning?" Travis asked before sipping his coffee.

"Nope. She's got a later shift. You should come by for dinner," Katarina answered.

Juan nudged Travis and his friend just smiled bashfully.

Katarina picked up their ticket and their payment. As she walked away, she heard the men scooting back their chairs, ready to go to work. Juan tipped his cowboy hat before disappearing out the front door with his friends, the bell over the door chiming softly. She finished ringing up their transaction and was thankful for the huge tip they had left her. Tucking it into her apron, she mentally added it to her slowly growing savings.

Of course, her savings would most likely end up paying for her mother's expenses, but she allowed herself a little dream of one day going on a real vacation to somewhere fancy like Cancun *without* her bitter mother. Maybe it was foolish to even consider the money hers to begin with. The *only* reason her mother had even allowed her to get a job was because they needed more money. Though the financial crunch was anxiety-inducing, it had liberated Katarina from the confines of her mother's home.

Even though she was twenty-eight, she lived at home with her elderly ailing mother. Katarina had been conceived for the sole purpose of taking care of her parents after the last of their children had left home. This truth had been instilled in her head since birth. Her parents made sure that she understood that college, marriage, and children were not in the cards for her life. Isolated from the world, Katarina's entire life until she was twenty-seven was her bitter, emotionally-remote parents and their stuffy home. Then her father had passed away and her mother had demanded that Katarina find a way to financially support her.

Earning her own money waitressing was the biggest accomplishment of her life. She was good at the job and she often wondered if it was her only talent. Sometimes she dreamed about having her own small place and making decisions for her own life, but knew it would never happen while her mother was still alive. Her mother's sharp tongue was very adept at keeping Katarina trapped in a web of guilt and fear.

Katarina both envied and resented her much older siblings for escaping the clutches of their parents and Ashley Oaks. She doubted she would ever escape.

Snagging the coffee pot, Katarina began to weave her way around the restaurant refilling cups and giving customers their tickets. She could see Randall eating and watching her out of the corner of her eye. It made her uneasy.

Her mother and father never let her have friends or boyfriends growing up. After school, she had to always go straight home to a long list of chores. Katarina didn't even have a friend until she started working at the cafe. Maybe Brenda didn't even count since they never hung out outside of work hours, but the other waitress was the closest thing Katarina had ever had to a friend. Her mother hated Brenda. She was convinced that Brenda was turning Katarina against her. Katarina didn't agree. It was Brenda who helped her see the world in a new way. It wasn't just about being her mother's constant caretaker, but about enjoying all that life had to offer. She supposed it was lucky that she was able to go to work after her father's death, otherwise she would have never even dared dream about one day doing something for herself. And if not for Brenda, Katarina wouldn't have found out that her wariness about Randall was justified.

Randall was just like her mother. They liked to hurt and dominate people they considered weaker than themselves.

As she poured him some coffee, Randall lightly touched her hip. "Getting skinny. You know I like women with something to hold on to."

She cocked her hip away from him, avoiding his touch as she finished pouring. "I work hard here and at home."

"I'd like you to work hard somewhere else," Randall said in that disconcerting tone of his.

Slapping the ticket down on the table, she plastered a fake smile on her face. "I'll take care of that when you're ready."

"I'd like to take care of you when you're ready," Randall said with a wide, yet mirthless smile.

Whipping about, Katarina hurried away, wishing Brenda hadn't taken a different shift. She had to cover the entire restaurant since Jolene was out sick. Usually Brenda traded tables with her so that Randall couldn't harass her.

Katarina took the orders from a new table and hurried behind the counter. She glanced over into the kitchen where the cooks were busy making breakfast as their Tejano music blasted away, covering the din of the costumers talking. She rang the bell and handed the order over to one of the cooks. She had a few minutes before she had to circle the restaurant again. Picking up a cleaver instead of a knife, she began to slice up some lemons, keeping one eye on the tables as she worked. She was feeling a little aggressive and the cleaver felt heavy and powerful in her grip. The lemon juice bit at her sinuses, but she liked the smell. It was a clean scent. She kept slicing and sweeping the pieces into a bowl. The restaurant always needed a lot of lemon for sweet tea during lunch time.

Randall raised his hand, money in his grip. He beckoned her over, smiling mockingly.

Sighing, she set the cleaver down and wiped off her hands. Just a few more seconds of him being a jerk and she would be free of him for another week or so. Scooting around the serving counter, she headed toward his table.

The bell over the front door jingled as it opened.

"Just find a table and I'll be right with you," Katarina called out, waving her hand.

A gasp from a customer pulled her attention away from Randall's wide grin. A man stood in the doorway, his hands pressed against his throat. His mouth opening and closing silently, he stumbled forward. Eyes wide with fear, he slowly reached out toward the customers that were staring at him in shock. Sinking down to his knees, the man violently coughed, blood pouring out of his mouth. Katarina rushed toward him, almost tripping over someone's purse. Randall arrived at the man's side before her.

The wounded man's hands were covered in blood as he pawed at Randall, imploring him silently for help. Katarina gasped at the horrible bloody mangled wreck beneath his chin. As silently as he had entered, the man fell forward as his eyes rolled up into his head. Randall barely caught the man by the shoulders and lowered him to the floor.

"Someone slit his throat or something!" Randall shouted. "Call 911!"

Customers stood in clusters around their tables in shocked silence, staring at the spectacle before them. One or two pulled out their phones. Katarina grabbed a small hand towel from her waistband and thrust it at Randall.

"I-I think you need to put pressure on his neck," she stammered.

Crouched in the growing pool of the wounded man's blood, Randall took the towel without a nasty word or leering look. With surprising gentleness, he pressed the rolled up cloth to the man's throat. "I don't know if this can help. Is there a doctor or nurse here?"

Hovering over the two men, Katarina shoved her frizzy bangs out of her face. She didn't know what to do. Her mind was racing and she couldn't think straight. The customers were slowly tiptoeing up around her, trying to see better, offering advice in distressed voices.

A few headed for the door.

"Hey, you can't leave! The sheriff is going to want to question us," Katarina called out.

The customers hesitated, then retreated to their seats.

"I don't think he's breathing no more," Randall said. "Did someone call 911?"

"I'm trying. No one is answering," someone replied.

Katarina crouched and touched the wounded man's wrist gently. She checked for a pulse with quivering fingers. She felt nothing.

"I think he's dead," she whispered, her voice catching on the words.

The man rose and bit into Randall's wrist in one swift motion. It happened so fast that Katarina registered the blood spraying her before she fully realized what had happened.

Randall's screams filled the cafe as people started to shout and cry out in alarm. Katarina was hit with another spray of blood as the man ripped a huge chunk of flesh from Randall's arm and chewed it.

The horror of the moment froze her body and seized her mind. Her heartbeat throbbed in her ears as she watched the bloodied man eating the meat torn from Randall's body.

"Help me," Randall gasped, struggling to escape.

The clearly insane man attacked again, teeth sinking into skin and muscle as Randall screamed.

Fear disintegrated into something cold and hard inside of Katarina's mind. She knew exactly what she needed to do. Twisting around, Katarina shoved her way through the chairs, bodies, and tables blocking her path. People's faces were twisted into screams and tables and chairs clattered to the floor as they tried to flee. Katarina stumbled a few times, but made it to the counter before the stampede to the back door exit could catch her. Leaning over the counter, she grabbed the cleaver.

Randall's screams became shriller as dreadful fleshy, ripping noises emanated from the front of the restaurant. Katarina ran toward the sound, her hand raised over her head. Men, women, and a few children ducked out of her way as she descended on the bloody chaos before the front door. Randall lay on the floor, his body seizing as the man tore at his face with his teeth.

Katarina felt strangely disconnected from the world around her as she brought the cleaver down with all her strength. It struck the back of the man's head with a meaty *thwack*. She attacked again and again.

It wasn't until the man lay silent at her feet, his head a butchered ruin, that Katarina felt fear and despair fill her.

She had just killed someone.

A sob broke free from her lips as she gaped at Randall. He was quiet now, not moving. She was covered in blood and bits of flesh and bone. It was warm and sticky.

Turning, she saw a few customers grouped near the back door staring at her in horror. One of them held his phone up to his ear.

"I saw it, hon. You did what you had to. I'll tell the police," the man with the phone said. "Pure self-defense."

A growl drew her attention to Randall just as a hand clasped her ankle. Randall rolled onto his side, his teeth gnashing as murky eyes glowered at her. Slipping in the blood, he tried to hold onto her while getting to his knees.

"Let go!" Katarina stepped back and tried to pull free.

She almost slipped and managed to grab a table, keeping herself upright. His grip did not lessen, but tightened. Growling again, Randall slid around in the blood as he tried to crawl toward her.

Katarina toppled a chair onto him, but Randall did not relent. He growled and snapped his teeth together, his teeth drawing ever closer to her leg.

"Let go of me!" Katarina raised the cleaver over her head. "Let go!"

Randall lunged, teeth snapping. She slammed the cleaver downward. Her first whack sliced off his nose and lips, but he kept trying to bite her, undeterred. She immediately hacked at his head again and kept hitting him until his fingers loosened and he fell silent.

She had killed Randall.

She had killed two men.

In a daze, she circled toward the back of the café and saw that no one remained inside. She was alone.

Feeling sick to her stomach, yet resolved, she walked over shattered dishes, clumps of food, past overturned chairs and tables, and out the back door into the sunlight.

The parking lot was nearly empty.

Reaching into her pocket, she pulled out the keys to her mother's old Ford Buick. She had to go home. Wash off the blood. Call the police. She had to tell them she had killed two men.

Unlocking the car door, she listened to the birds singing in the trees. The morning was so peaceful. Yet it felt like it was apart from her. She stood outside the world, as though nothing was real in this moment except the blood covering her and the cleaver in her hand.

Once behind the wheel, she tossed the cleaver onto the passenger seat and started the car. It slowly rolled out of the parking lot and down a sun-dappled lane. The cafe was on the outskirts of Ashley Oaks, so she drove along the old highway until she could turn onto a city street.

The blood on her reeked, coppery and disgusting. She ignored her discomfort, concentrating on driving home. There she would have to deal with her mother screaming at her and demanding to know what had happened.

And she would have to answer truthfully.

She had killed two men.

If only she felt some other emotion other than eerily calm.

As she turned down another street, she saw the town clinic's parking lot packed with cars. Wounded were being carried inside by concerned friends and family. One woman was screaming, clutching a bloody stump where her hand used to be. Several of the Sherriff department deputies attempted to direct the human traffic making their way inside. The crowd was loud, terrified, and shell-shocked.

Katarina observed the chaotic scene as her car slid past the clinic. The wounded people reminded her of the man staggering into the café. Something was wrong. Terribly, terribly wrong.

Just as she turned onto another street, she heard screams erupting from the direction of the clinic. A few moments later there were gunshots.

Clutching the steering wheel, Katarina stared out at the world dispassionately. Everything felt dream-like and unreal. Cars sped past her as gunshots continued to bark and echo through the neighborhood. She spotted a woman standing in a side street screaming.

Another turn.

Another shocking scene.

A car crashed into a tree. Bloodied people clawing at the windows. The engine on fire.

Chaos was everywhere. Even on her own street.

Ahead was her home.

No, not her home.

It was her mother's house and Katarina's prison.

In the front yard, Katarina's mother stood in her nightgown, clutching the garden hose. She was screaming at two children racing through her flower garden, brandishing the spray nozzle like a gun. She always sprayed dogs, cats, children and even adults to keep them off her perfectly-manicured lawn.

But Katarina knew that the two children would not run away from the blast of water. They were ruined masses of flesh just like the stranger and Randall.

She tried to cry out and warn her mother, but her voice was lost in her throat.

In seconds, the children were upon her, knocking the nozzle from her hand.

Katarina braked, shifted into park, grabbed the cleaver, and sprang from the car.

This isn't real, she thought, but the cleaver in her hand was sticky with blood and fleshy bits.

The world didn't feel real, but the cleaver did.

It wasn't until she was hacking away at the small limbs and heads of the children biting into her mother's chest that the world finally snapped back into focus. Suddenly every whack of the cleaver registered fully in her senses: the impact that jarred her joints, the terrible sound of the blade slashing through flesh and bone, and the stink of death and blood.

Sobbing, she kicked the bodies of the children away from her mother. The tiny broken forms lay silent and twisted on the green lawn.

"Mother, I'm so sorry," Katarina cried out.

Leaning over her mother, she saw the woman's angry eyes fastened on her with seething hate. The woman who had conceived her to be her servant, her caretaker, glared at her with unremorseful hate.

"I'll take care of you, mother," Katarina promised.

The hateful gaze faded into oblivion.

"I'll always take care of you."

Katarina raised her cleaver.

In the darkened house, Katarina listened to the world dying. Showered, dressed in jeans, a t-shirt, and denim jacket, she heard the moans of the dead mingling with the death cries of the living outside the tiny house.

The TV was muted, but the closed captioning and scenes of chaos told the full story. Something terrible was happening in the world and it was everywhere.

As she stared at the images of death and destruction, she loaded her father's old hunting rifle. The cleaver was cleaned and lying on the coffee table beside a box of ammunition. A backpack filled with her meager possessions listed near the front door. Where she going she didn't know, but she would not sit in this house any longer. It had never been a home. It had been her prison. And now, as the world died, she was set free.

Standing, she shoved the box of ammunition into her jacket. She stared at the cleaver and its brutal, shiny beauty. She started to reach for it, but reconsidered. The intimacy of killing with it was too much to bear.

She snagged her backpack on the way out the door.

The car sat where she had left it, the driver's door open, the engine still ticking. One of the things that used to be a living being rushed her. She paused in her steps, raised her rifle, gazed through the sight, and fired. A plume of blood flashed bright red in the sunlight, then it fell.

She had killed three men, two children, and her mother today.

A quick look inside the car and she saw it was clear. She slid into the driver's seat, shut the door, and shifted gears. Black smoke was rising from the direction of the highway. She would head out of town and see if anywhere in the world was safe.

A stop sign loomed ahead and she considered running it. At the last minute, she banged on her brakes and stared through the windshield at the quiet street before her. It looked so normal, quaint, and peaceful, but it was a lie. Death was everywhere now. The world she had known was dying.

She started the car through the intersection when she heard the whoop of a siren. Her foot stomped on the brake.

A deputy sheriff's car pulled up beside her. The window scrolled down and she quickly lowered hers as well. A very young man with blond hair and bright blue eyes that were a little too wide stared out at her.

"You need to get to city hall! We're making a perimeter to keep them out!" he yelled at her. "I'm heading there now. Want to come along?"

She killed the engine, grabbed her rifle and her backpack, and abandoned her mother's car. The deputy shoved the passenger door open and she climbed in. The car reeked of sweet and blood. The young man was shaking and looked more like a scared boy than a seasoned lawman. He was covered in blood.

"You okay?" she asked warily.

"Not my blood," he answered sadly.

"I'm Katarina."

"Curtis," he said, and shifted gears.

The car glided through town in the direction of the big hotel that loomed over Ashley Oaks. Empty store fronts, abandoned gas stations, and forlorn, empty lots were once the telltale signs of the dying town. But now it was truly dead.

Or was it?

Ahead, Katarina saw trucks filled with earth pulled up around the new construction site. A group of men were shoving heavy bags of cement and dirt under the vehicles and between the cabs and the trailers creating a barricade. A mangled wreck was near the new fortifications.

"That's it?" Katarina asked.

"Yeah," Curtis responded in a tired, frightened voice.

They parked on a side street and ran together to the blocked off area. As they scrambled over the back of a truck, the construction site came into focus. People were camped inside, clustered together. She could see some of her old customers among the survivors: Juan, Travis, Old Man Watson, Peggy the city secretary, Mayor Reyes, and others.

Katarina felt the world tilt and shift again as the world took on a new reality.

A shout behind her drew her attention. Turning, she saw some of the construction workers scrambling to evade one of the dead things. Raising her rifle, she felt a tear on her cheek as she did what she now knew she was very good at and would serve her well in this new world.

She killed.

The Unknowns' Story

This untold tale is about the people who dwell in the background of the AS THE WORLD DIES trilogy. Not everyone survived to make it to the fort, and not every survivor in Texas made it to Ashley Oaks. I have been dying for some time to tell some of those stories.

The inception of this particular story occurred when a small press asked me to be a part of a new flash fiction anthology. I wrote the first section of this story with that anthology in mind. Later, when the anthology was canceled, I decided to expand the story for my online fans now that I was free of the constraints of word limits.

The tale is rather disturbing as it deals with vengeance, jealousy, and madness in the claustrophobic confines of a survivor haven.

I am very happy to include *A Terrible Moment* in this collection.

A Terrible Moment

She wanted it to be over.

The constant moaning of the dead outside the warehouse was wearing away at her last nerve. Her hands trembled at her sides as she clenched them into tight fists. The cool air reeked of rotting citrus, but at least it kept the stench of the dead at bay.

Nearby, she could see her soon to be ex-husband, his trollop secretary, and the plant manager engaged in a heated discussion. They had invited her to join their planning session, but she had declined. She wanted nothing to do with them.

She was only here because of her children. The kids were with their lousy father when the dead had risen. In a panic, she had sped across town to this godforsaken orange juice factory, just to end up trapped with the man she loathed and his slut.

Looking over her shoulder, she saw the kids playing with toys the whore had given them. The two boys happily chatted as they played, oblivious to everything around them. They had no idea that their father was a cheating bastard and that the woman they called Aunt Julie was a fucking bitch. They didn't understand how much pain she was in and maybe they wouldn't even care. They worshipped their father. That thought only fed her rage.

She looked at the glass venetian blinds covering the window next to her. She could barely make out the outline of the dead creatures gathered outside her hellish prison. Fortunately, the iron burglar bars over the windows kept the zombies out, but they also trapped her inside.

The stench of slowly decomposing citrus was so terrible she pulled the collar of her gray sweatshirt over her nose. It was stained and worn. But then again, so was she. After marrying, she had hacked off her long tawny tresses, tossed out the makeup, and settled into a comfortable life of being a mother and wife. She had done everything she could for the good-for-nothing and now he was divorcing her.

Scowling, she observed her husband as he spoke passionately to the other two adults. Some stupid plan about climbing onto the roof and lowering everyone down onto a truck with a rope was taking form. They were all idiots.

"We can break the windshield, crawl in, and get it started. Yeah, that will be a little dangerous, but the truck is high enough off the ground that they won't be able to reach us. They don't climb. We've seen that," her husband said.

She scoffed at his words. He always had to be in charge. What made him think he was the big hero now?

Annoyed, she took a step closer to the window. The blinds were stuck and not completely closed. A chewed-up face with one eye missing growled at her as it pressed against the bars.

The laughter of the kids as they played angered her. They believed their father would save them. They weren't even paying attention to her. They didn't care about her and her pain.

Rage burned in her soul.

They all thought they were so safe behind these bars. What was worse was that they all believed her stupid husband could actually save them from the hungry mouths of the walking dead. It disgusted her how her kids believed their daddy was so wonderful. She was the one who always took care of them. She was the one who gave them life.

Discreetly, she slipped her fingers over the edge of the blind slat, wagging them in the face of the zombie.

It snapped its jaws at her.

A dark and evil, yet wonderful idea unfurled in her mind. It pushed through her red hot anger and spread through her like cold water.

Glancing over her shoulder, she glowered at the happy little scene of her children playing in the shadow of their father. How easily they ignored her. How easily they pretended she didn't matter. That she didn't exist.

How dare they ignore her.

She returned her gaze to the snapping teeth, her fingers scant inches from their broken edges.

Yes, it could be over. A little bite and her troubles would be done. Just a little nip on the end of a finger. No one would notice until it was too late.

And then they would not be able to ignore her. They would all see that her stupid husband's plan would fail.

They would all die.

She pushed her fingertips closer to the desperate mouth of the zombie.

Alan was tired. Tired to the very marrow of his bones. Every muscle in his body ached and his head was pounding. Yet, it didn't matter. He had to stay alert. He had to keep going. He had to find a way to save the people who were depending on him. He had to save his kids.

The smell of rotting citrus burned his nostrils as he spoke with the others about a possible escape route. The decaying fruit kept at bay the reek of the dead outside the chained factory doors. He wasn't sure which was worse: the smell of the shambling, ravenous dead or the slowly-decomposing oranges in the crates.

Nearby, his two boys were playing with truck models that Julie, his secretary, had given them. The small trucks sported the logos of the orange juice companies to which the factory had provided juice until the dead decided to get up and attack the living. The models had sat on shelf in his office for years, but now they were the only toys his children possessed. The twins always played well together and he could hear Parker explaining to Hunter that the binder clips from Julie's desk were zombies and they had to run them over with the trucks and squish them. Meanwhile, Alice, his baby girl, was asleep on the sofa in his office. He could see her through the open doorway. Her little pink mouth was pursed in her sleep and one little hand was tucked up by her tawny curls.

Nearby, the wife he had been divorcing sulked in a dark corner of the big building. They had invited Debbie to join their planning session, but her response had been "I don't want to be around your slut secretary."

Julie had almost burst into tears, but he had pulled her away before his ex could unleash more venom.

Now, as they tried to plan a way to get out, he felt ill at ease. Something was amiss.

Rob, the big burly plant manager, scowled slightly. He rubbed his scruffy beard with one hand as he considered the plan. "So we climb down using ropes, huh? That may be tough on the kids and the women folk."

"They'll have to go first. We'll have to lower them," Alan explained. "Then we'll follow."

"I don't know if I like the idea of standing on the back of a truck with the kids and..." Julie's eyes flicked to the figure standing in the shadows near the windows. She lowered her voice. "She's so mean and erratic."

"Do you think she'll cooperate?" Rob didn't look him in the eye.

Debbie was a difficult subject for Alan, and people tried to avoid speaking about her in a direct manner to him. It was almost as if they were afraid if they spoke of her, she would descend on them like a summoned demon. She was embarrassingly-bold with her nasty temper.

Alan pondered the question before shrugging his big shoulders. "I don't know. But I don't think she'll hurt the kids."

"But what about Julie? She's convinced you're having an affair with her. She's irrational about it," Rob pointed out. "How many times did she drive down here to cause a scene?"

"She even said that my baby isn't my husband's, but yours," Julie whispered, tears threatening again.

Julie was a tiny thing, pretty as could be, and often too sweet for her own good. It made all the men at the factory want to protect her. Seeing her with tears in her eyes brought out the big brother in Alan. He put an arm around her and gave her a little squeeze.

"Don't you worry about your little one, Julie. Your mama and your husband are taking care of your baby. I know it. And don't let Debbie get to you. She's been accusing me of fooling around since the day we got married," Alan said.

Julie stared up at him with her enormous brown eyes and sniffled loudly. "You think my baby and Tony are alive?"

Alan lied to keep her calm. "Yes, I do."

"You could at least keep your hands off of her in front of the kids!" Debbie's venomous voice raked him like a claw.

Dropping his arm, Alan slowly turned to face the woman he had once loved. She was wearing her usual uniform of stained sweat pants, a faded t-shirt, battered loafers and a hoodie. He hadn't realized until today how much he avoided looking at her directly, but he forced himself to study her face. Her blue eyes seemed too wide and gleeful above her pale, tight lips. Instead of the long tawny tresses that had fluttered around her shoulders during their courtship, her hair was cut very short. Nothing about her seemed feminine anymore. Nor was she particularly manly. In that moment, she reminded him of the mythological harpy. She was always so ready to pluck out his heart.

"He was just comforting a friend," Rob dared to say.

"Really? Is that what we call slut whores now?" Debbie asked sharply. "Friends?"

"Could you not speak like that in front of the children?" Alan asked in a soft voice, trying to calm her.

The boys were staring in their direction, both of them wide-eyed with their mouths slightly hanging open.

"Why? So they won't know what an asshole their father is? So they won't know he's going around and fucking his secretary? So they won't know that their father is a fucking douchebag who cheats on his wife?"

"How can you be so mean?" Julie exclaimed. She pressed a trembling hand to her chest, her eyes wide. "How?"

Debbie smirked at Julie. "Mean? You call this mean after what you've done?"

"Enough of this," Alan said shortly. He was barely keeping his temper.

One of the main reasons he had been divorcing his wife was because on more than one occasion, she had driven him so far into a rage he had wanted to hurt her. It had become more difficult over time to endure her verbal abuse, but her physical attacks were the last straw. When she had knocked him out with a frying pan after accusing him of cheating on her with Julie, that was the last straw. He had woken up to the children crying over him, thinking he was dead as Debbie nonchalantly made dinner.

"We're getting out of here, Debbie. We are sorting out the details now, but we're going to get out of here and find somewhere safe with supplies for the kids. Can you help us?" Alan looked at the disheveled woman beside him, willing her to be cooperative.

Her hands tucked into her hoodie, Debbie shrugged. "I need a nap."

"Fine," Alan sighed.

"Glad to get your permission," Debbie snarled, then strode into the office. She picked up her baby girl, placed her on the floor with a pillow, and spread out on the sofa.

"I need to feed the baby soon," Julie whispered.

"She hasn't caught on?" Rob asked, raising his eyebrows.

"No," Alan answered. "We've been out of formula for three days and she hasn't said a word about the baby needing to be fed. She has no clue Julie's been breastfeeding Alice." Alan's mouth drew into a hard line. Debbie had stopped breastfeeding Alice within a month of her birth. She complained that it was too much work. It was good fortune that Julie was breastfeeding and willing to feed the six-month-old baby. It touched Alan's heart every time he saw Julie holding Alice. He knew how hard it must be when she didn't know the fate of her own child.

"How can a mama not know that? What is wrong with her?" Rob shook his head.

Alan shrugged. "No clue. She wouldn't go to the doctor." He rubbed the scruff on his chin with agitation and glanced over at his boys. They had returned to playing with muted enthusiasm.

"I'll see what I can do about the rope or a ladder to get down to the back of a truck," Rob said finally. "We have to get out of here before we're totally out of food."

"Strange saying that in an orange juice factory," Julie sighed. She rubbed her nose and looked into the office warily. "What if she tries to shove me off the truck or something?"

"I don't think she'd go that far," Alan assured Julie. "She's bitter, but she's not homicidal."

Rob sighed. "You better hope not. We got enough trouble with those zombies out there. I'll be back." The big guy took off across the concrete floor, his head down.

They were all weary. The zombies outside, coupled with Debbie's rants, had them all on edge. Julie watched Rob walk away. Her big eyes were rimmed with tears again.

Laying her hand gently on Alan's arm, she whispered, "We could leave her..."

"No. No. She may be...sick. But we can't do that. We can't." Alan shook his head adamantly. "I can't do that to her or the kids."

Shoving her thick brown hair back from her face, Julie took a deep breath. She looked warily toward the open office door. "As soon as she's asleep, I'll go get Alice so I can feed her." Her fingers played with the buttons of her blouse and her faraway expression said it all. Julie was thinking of her own child that was somewhere out there in the dead lands.

Alan seriously doubted if many people were still alive, but he didn't want to upset Julie by saying so. After giving her a gentle hug, he walked back to where his boys were playing. Squatting down, he kissed their foreheads.

"You can be this truck," Parker informed him, handing him a model.

"Okay! Let's smash those zombies," Alan said, the tightness in his chest alleviating as he felt the love and trust of his children wash over him.

Around twenty minutes later, he saw Julie slip into the office and gently pick up the sleeping baby. Looking away to give her privacy, he continued to play with the twins. They were lying on their stomachs, propped on one elbow as the model trucks plowed through the binder clip zombies over and over again.

Julie's terrified scream rang through the building, making the kids gasp as Alan leaped to his feet. Looking into the office, he saw Julie clutching Alice to her breasts with one arm as she shoved his office chair at Debbie with the other. Debbie was lashing out, trying to grab Alice. The baby was screaming, her face red as she cried.

"Debbie, leave her alone! She's trying to help Alice!" Alan rushed into the office grabbed Debbie's arm and yanked her about.

Debbie's eyes were devoid of life. Her teeth snapped as she lunged toward him. Alan cried out in shock, but managed to get his elbow up, slam it into her neck, and knock her away. He stumbled back a few feet mortified at what he was seeing, his mind a mix of emotions, primarily confusion.

How had this happened?

"Boys, run!" Alan ordered.

"Watch out!" Julie screamed.

The patter of their sneakers against the concrete floor was a small comfort as Debbie lunged at him again. He caught her arms and shoved her. She hit the doorjamb and fell into the office on her hands and knees. Alice's cries were desperate and Julie tried to calm her as she sought refuge behind Alan's big desk. He darted forward and kicked Debbie, knocking her to the floor.

The zombie got her hands under her body and scrambled toward the desk with terrifying speed. Julie cried out in terror, darting into the far corner, her body turned to protect Alice. Alan looked around frantically for a weapon and grabbed his office chair. Lifting it up, he brought it down hard on Debbie, pinning her under it. The zombie's body thrashed about, trying to get up. Leaning all his weight onto the chair, Alan pinned the snarling creature.

"Get out, Julie! Get out!"

Skirting the desk, Julie ran out of the room, clutching Alice to her chest. Alan struggled to keep Debbie restrained, but she was relentless in her attempt to escape. Unexpectedly, she managed to get a hand under her chest and shoved upwards with a mighty push. Alan lost his grip on the chair and it crashed over onto its side. He ran out of the office, slamming the door behind him. With shaking fingers, he drew out his keys and locked it.

The sound of running feet and the jangle of keys startled him. He whirled about to see Rob darting around the silent conveyor belts toward him.

"What's going on?"

Alan gestured to Debbie as she beat on the thick glass set in the door. Her mouth was pulled back in a grimace as her teeth snapped together. As he stared at her hands, he realized what had happened with terrible clarity. He felt his chest tighten with despair and anger.

"She let one of them bite her," he gasped.

"What?" Rob studied Debbie in shock. "What the hell? She's a zombie?"

"Look at the tip of her middle finger! That's a bite! When she was over in that damn corner, I bet she let one of them bite her!"

"Why would she *do* that?" Julie demanded. "Why? That doesn't make any sense!"

Alan felt tears of anger burning in his eyes. "Because she hates me that much. She wanted to turn so she could....Oh, God! She was willing to kill the boys!"

"Where are they?" Julie looked around nervously. "Hunter! Parker!"

The twins darted out from behind some machinery and latched onto Julie. Alice continued to cry, her tiny face contorted in anger and terror. Julie tried to shush her, her hands still trembling.

"I say it's time to go," Rob said. "She'll break out of there soon."

"Yeah," Alan agreed. "Yeah. Boys, we need to go."

Parker and Hunter, too wise for their mere seven years, picked up their toys and walked to his side.

"Do we have to leave Mama?" Hunter asked, looking uncertain.

"She's a monster now," Parker decided, staring at his dead mother.

"She always was," Rob muttered.

"Yeah, boys. We need to go. Your mother…well, she's one of those things now. We gotta go without her." Alan rubbed their shoulders with his trembling hands.

"Okay," the boys answered together. They both were pensive, but seemed to understand.

"Come on, boys. Time to go!" Rob said, guiding the children away.

"Let's go," Alan said, reaching out to guide Julie toward the stairs that led up to the roof.

Alice's cries had settled into a hiccupping sob. The baby snuggled under Julie's chin, gripping the collar of her blouse with a tiny hand. Julie peered up at Alan, her eyes full of fear and resignation. "Where are we going?"

As they walked swiftly after Rob and the boys, Alan glanced back at his dead wife. She was slamming her head into the glass of the door, desperately trying to get out.

"The Madison Mall," he said at last. "We'll be safe there."

They left the floor of the orange juice factory, climbing toward the roof, leaving behind the undead version of his former wife, snarling, hissing, and slamming her hands against the door. Sadly, he realized, she wasn't much different in death than she had been in life.

Stepping out onto the roof, he closed the door behind him.

Ken and Lenore's Story

Ken and Lenore have always been fan favorites since they appeared on the online serial. They enter the story in FIGHTING TO SURVIVE and have important roles in SIEGE. Their friendship was always one of my favorite elements of the story.

I started their *first day* story online, but I could never figure out the end of their tale. Because I'm an organic writer, I trust the stories to tell themselves through the characters. This time, I was completely blocked. The story remained unfinished for two years.

It wasn't until I was done with the SIEGE revisions for the Tor edition that I was able to write on this story again. By the time I finished, I realized why I had to wait to uncover the ending. This story and Siege are perfect companion pieces. Together they bring the story of Ken and Lenore full circle and are a wonderful testament to their loving friendship.

Friendship in the Time of Zombies

1.
Lenore

The alarm clock's annoying scream woke Lenore from her deep slumber and she growled with irritation. Slapping her hand down on the top of the already-battered electric alarm clock, she stared at the blinking red letters grimly.

Seven o'clock.

She hated seven o'clock before the big *spring forward* time change. It was still dark outside and it didn't seem right to be getting out of bed before the sun rose. Of course, in just another week that would change and she'd be getting up to bright sunlight and singing birds. But for now, like she had all through the fall and winter, she sat up in bed to be greeted by a cold room and silence.

Feeling grumpy, she threw off her covers and slid to her feet. The furniture in her room was antique and a bit battered. It was what they could save after Hurricane Rita had flattened their old home in Jefferson County. Two trees had taken down their massive Victorian during the storm and not much had been left to salvage.

"Didn't wanna pay to get the plumbing fixed anyway," her grandmother had sniffed when they had come from the rescue shelter and seen what had happened to the old home.

Lenore stared into the mirror over her vanity and frowned. She was a big girl with dark skin and eyes. Her hair was short, to her chin, and straightened. Fussing with her bangs, she sighed. She had been trying to emulate Halle Berry. A bad move. A girl at the beauty school had offered to do her hair and had done a good job frying it. Though Lenore had a firm rule not to let a white woman do her hair, they had been in a class on how to do hairstyles for African-Americans and she had thought it would be okay. Her over-processed hair was breaking off at the tips as the result. She wasn't sure what she was going to do with her hair next. She'd have to study the new hairstyle magazines at the beauty parlor. It would have to be a radical move. She'd have to cut it almost to the scalp and restart.

With a frown and a grunt, she padded into the kitchen that was directly across from her bedroom. Already an enormous feast was on the table. Her grandmother, Ethel Mae, was used to cooking for a large group of people and had yet to adjust to the fact it was just the two of them now. After the hurricane had come on shore, flattened Sabine Pass, and torn apart the towns in Jefferson County, Lenore's grandmother had decided she was done and moved them out West. That meant leaving most of their huge family behind. Lenore's aunts, uncles and cousins had always been at her grandmother's huge Victorian even though they technically didn't live there. It was a big adjustment for both of them now that they lived far away from the rest of the family.

Staring at the massive display of food, Lenore wondered if her grandmother expected her to eat it all. She stood in the kitchen's small dining area and peeked through the archway into the living room located in the front of the house. Her grandmother was watching the morning news. As usual, she was dressed in a flowered dress, fluffy slippers, and had her white hair in a neat bun.

"You better get to eating. You're up late again," her grandmother called out.

Lenore scowled and slid into a chair. Her grandmother considered anytime after 5:30 AM to be getting up late. Serving herself some grits, bacon and fried eggs, she yawned loudly. She grabbed a fresh biscuit from the pile in an old basket on the table and bit into it. The wonderful taste and warmth made her feel a little more awake.

"Got a bunch of people doing some really crazy stuff down Houston way. Hope your Uncle Bo is on the road and not around there. I hate it when Negroes all go crazy. Makes the rest of us look bad."

"Grandma, we're black or African-American. Stop calling us Negroes," Lenore corrected her grumpily. It was an old argument and it made her surly.

"I'm a Negro. I'm not no African-American. I am not from Africa. I was born and raised in Port Arthur, Texas and I am an American citizen of these United States. I am no black person neither. I have brown skin..."

Her grandmother continued on and Lenore shoved a huge mouthful of grits in her mouth to keep from sassing back. She tapped her fork lightly against the edge of the plate and waited for her grandmother to be done.

"Oh, Lord Jesus, they're eating each other!"

Lenore frowned. "Who is?"

"Them crazy Negroes in Houston!"

"Black people-"

"Stop correcting me!"

Lenore heaved herself up out of the chair, pulled her Tweety Bird T-shirt down over her stomach, and plodded over into the living room. "Nobody is out eating nobody."

Her grandmother twisted around in her lazy boy and glared at her. "Do not tell me I'm lying, young woman. I'll slap you good."

Lenore almost rolled her eyes then saw the footage being fed live from Houston. At first it looked like a riot or a bunch of black people on a looting spree (which always made her cringe), but then she realized most of the people rampaging were covered in blood and had terrible wounds. The news camera was aiming down the street as the rioters surged toward them. Innocent bystanders were being dragged down onto the street and it sure did look like the crazy looters were biting them.

"Gotta be gangbangers on some bad crack or something," Lenore said.

"Bunch of crazy sons of bitches," her grandmother decided and thumped her armrest. "Now they're gonna get all shot up and it's gonna look bad. We'll end up with that crazy Al Shaprton pretending he's Martin Luther King. I could slap that boy."

Lenore sighed softly and shook her head. "You know how it is, Grandma."

Her grandmother scowled deeply and glared at the TV. "Their mamas should go down there and whoop on them for doing such crazy stuff on the TV. Not right. Not right."

Lenore didn't want to see anymore of the mayhem from Houston. She was angry enough with the media for their complete dismissal of Hurricane Rita's devastation in East Texas. When it had not hit Houston and Galveston, the media acted like it was a close call and moved on to the next news story. It was not another Katrina, so why should they care? Of course, to the people living in the small cities and towns of Jefferson County, it had been just as bad as Hurricane Katrina. In one fell swoop, the storm not only destroyed homes, but also lives and businesses. Lenore's family was still trying to recover and find new jobs. A lot of employers had just packed up and moved to other areas in Texas.

Lenore did not trust the news media and never would. If you paid attention to the news you'd believe every Hispanic in America was an illegal immigrant, every black man was in a gang, and all white men were serial killers or pedophiles. How women were portrayed wasn't much better. It was just better to live her life and not bother with the stupidity of people.

After a hot shower, Lenore dressed in her usual outfit of jeans, a white button down oxford blouse, her favorite leopard print jacket and her battered loafers. She tried to fuss with her hair, but it just annoyed her. It had to be changed and soon or she was going to go crazy. Kissing her fingertips, she pressed them to the photo of Common she had taped to her mirror and headed out the door.

"...telling you, Olympia, they are all crazy. On crack!" Her grandmother was on the phone with her best friend, Olympia Hernandez. Even though the old ladies lived within walking distance of each other, they preferred to sit in their La-z-Boys, watching the same shows, and discussing them on the phone. It was impossible to get through on the phone to either one of them during the soaps and talk shows.

Lenore leaned over and pressed a kiss to her grandmother's cheek. She got a pat on the cheek and a kiss, then her grandmother kept on complaining about the whacked out people eating each other in Houston.

"Maybe the government put something in the water," Lenore offered.

Her grandmother eyed her and then immediately repeated this to Olympia. "It's like the old crazy man on the public access is always talking about!"

Rolling her eyes, Lenore trudged to the front door, grabbed her huge leather bag, and headed out for another day of work at Ken's Diva Beauty Shop. As usual, she rode her bike and she rather enjoyed the briskness of the morning now that she was awake and fully clothed. The sun was just making an appearance over the hills, but her quaint little neighborhood was wide-awake and in full swing.

Already, old Mr. Thames was out in his yard working on his spring garden. She waved to him then swung around the corner to head into the downtown of Stross, Texas. It was not much of a town. The population consisted of old people or families with hardly any young people about. Most were smart and got out of town after high school. Her dream was to save up enough money to make it back to East Texas. Back to the bayou and the good old soul of the area. She missed the ocean. She missed the crawfish. She missed her house full of relatives. But her grandmother had raised her since her mama died and her daddy went out onto the oilrigs and she had felt obliged to come with her to this tiny forsaken town.

She was just parking her bike when Mr. Cloy, the man who ran the hardware store next to Ken's shop, arrived to unlock his door.

"Hey, Lenore. Howya doing?"

"Doing good, Mr. Cloy."

The skinny guy with too much black hair and the bushiest mustache in the world looked grim. "See the news?"

"'bout Houston?"

"That and all that rioting in Chicago. You know how that plane crashed yesterday?"

"News thought it was 9-11 all over again? Yep."

"Well, rumor is that there was something bad on that plane that is making people go crazy and kill each other. Chicago is bad. Wonder if it's Al Qaeda?"

"How does that explain Houston?" Lenore raised an eyebrow at him.

"Maybe they put something in the water," Mr. Cloy offered. "I dunno. It's got me on edge. Got me thinking that the world is going to hell fast. Damn Arabs with their Mohammad."

Lenore blinked at him, but didn't bother to argue. "Well, we're all the way out here away from everything and everybody. I don't see any of that crazy shit happening here," Lenore assured him.

"I hope so, Lenore." Mr. Cloy shook his head. "Crazy times, Lenore. It's the End Times."

"Well, if Jesus is coming back today I better do something with my hair," she said very deadpan.

Mr. Cloy was probably not really listening to her. "Yeah, End Times. We're seeing the last days." He shoved the door open and entered his store.

Lenore peered through the glass in the old wood door of the beauty shop and saw Ken busy on an early appointment's hair. He saw her and waved her in, smiling brightly. He was attractive with the tan skin of his Mexican mother and freckles of his Scot-Irish father. His eyes were a very pretty shade of brown with glints of gold and Lenore envied his tall, slim, fit physique. She felt short and squat next to him.

"Good morning, girlfriend!"

"Hey, Ken," she muttered as she walked past him.

"How are you?" He winked at her and she detected a tiny bit of makeup on his lids. Ken had trouble holding back at times and she could understand how hard it was for him to be a very out, very gay man in a small Texas town. The original owner of the shop had fooled the townspeople for years into thinking he was straight until he brought his very cute, very flamboyant boyfriend, Ken, to town. A year later, Ken's ex had abandoned him and the town for another man and left Ken with the shop. Lenore didn't know the entire story, but she knew that according to Ken, the former owner was a "cheating ass bitch of a boyfriend who deserved to die."

"Other than seeing people eating each other on the news, I'm fine," she answered.

"Eating how? Good or bad way?" Ken gave her a sly look.

"Bad. Like cannibals," she answered, deftly destroying his pornographic dreams.

"Ugh, that is why I so do not watch the news!" Ken frowned and began teasing the customer's hair into an even bigger, blonder poof.

"Well, it's all over the news," Lenore told him.

"Well, we just won't watch it today, will we? It's the E! channel all day today! Yay!"

Lenore rolled her eyes and went to turn on the TV at the back of the shop and set it to the right channel. They had left it on CNN the night before and she felt her stomach churn as the image on the screen was instantly of a massive riot with deranged people attacking a reporter. They were literally *biting* her.

"Freaks in Houston still going at it," she muttered to herself.

Right before she changed the channel, she saw that the footage was actually from Boston. A shiver of fear flowed down her spine and she hit the remote control to flip over to the entertainment network.

Standing up, she shoved the horrible image out of her mind. No time for news media crap. Time to work.

2.
Nothing As It Seems

Despite his wide smile and exuberance, Ken was having a very bad day. The no-good ex-boyfriend had called him early in the morning to tell him he was getting married in Canada. It had taken all of Ken's willpower not to burst into tears and scream at him. He had pretended to be happy and chatted away as though his heart hadn't just been ripped out and thrown out the window. What little hope he had that he would be reunited with Darryl, his lost love, had been summarily squashed.

But he was not going to let anyone know that he was hurting. He had a business to run. A small business in the middle of nowhere, Texas, but it was *his* beauty shop. It was going to be a good day one way or the other. He had prayed that God would grant him grace and a good attitude. Maybe it was a good ol' jolt of holy power or maybe just his grim determination, but he was smiling.

He checked his eyes for the millionth time to make sure they were not swollen or red from crying. He was satisfied that his expert makeup job to cover up the redness was looking brilliant. He continued to tease Mrs. Chentworth's hair into the biggest 'do in Texas and chattered on about all the latest gossip he had read that morning on the internet entertainment blogs.

Lenore was huffy again and that was fine by him. When his no good rotten cheating boyfriend had left him with the beauty shop and vanished for the glories of artsy Marfa, Texas, he had hired Lenore to help him build his clientele. The black population had grown since hurricanes Katrina and Rita sent evacuees fleeing into the small towns of Texas. Some had decided to stay and enjoy the good weather, down home hospitality and cheaper cost of living. Lenore was straight out of beauty school, but she was trained specifically to care for the hair of the black ladies. Since she had joined the shop, he had seen his appointment book swell. It hadn't taken long for her to become his daily verbal foil. She was Eeyore to his Tigger and that worked well for them. He loved work now, and he owed it to his grumpy girlfriend.

"Do you think he's sleeping with her?" his client asked about the latest "it" boy in Hollywood.

"Honey, he's gayer than I am!" Ken flashed a smile in her direction and covertly checked his eyes again. He still wanted to cry, but he would not. To try and cover how much he was hurting, he did a very flamboyant pose.

"Embracing the stereotype, Ken," Lenore drawled from across the shop as she checked in their latest shipment of hair extensions.

"This coming from the classic stereotype of the angry black woman?" Ken batted his eyelashes at her and returned to his poofing of Mrs. Chentworth's classic Texas bouffant.

Lenore harrumphed from across the room. "I ain't angry. I'm grumpy. There is a difference."

"You gonna get all sassy at me, snapping your fingers and flipping your weave?" Ken teased.

She glowered. "One, I ain't sassy. Two, the only one who snaps their fingers around here is you. Three, what I do with my weave is none of your damn business."

Ken stuck his tongue out at her.

Lenore dismissed him with a look and went back to work.

He chattered on to his customer as he worked and ignored the TV playing in the background. He always felt happier when he was working in the shop. He may have received it as a goodbye gift from his rich ex, but he had decorated to make it his own. The walls were a deep burgundy and decorated with lots of swanky artwork depicting hairstyles and fashions over the ages. Fresh flowers were tucked into hand-painted vases and soft trip hop music played in the background. He may have gotten stuck in Podunk, Nowhere, but he was doing the best he could to make it work.

When he finished with Mrs. Chentworth's hair, he took her check gratefully, waved to her as she walked out the door, tucked the check into the cash register, and burst into tears.

"What's wrong?" Lenore asked from across the shop.

"That bastard is getting married in Canada!"

"Oh," Lenore said, and then added matter-of-factly, "But he's no good for you."

"I know! I know! But all I wanted was a good husband, a nice home, my own beauty shop and...and..."

"One out of three ain't bad," Lenore reminded him.

Ken sniffled a little and shrugged. "I just thought he was the one."

Ken was always looking for the one. He had hid that he was gay quite successfully all through his childhood and into his teens until he had fallen madly in love with the student council president. On impulse he had written the boy a love letter. The next day his crush had read it over the school intercom and outed him in the most vicious manner possible. Ken had tried to sneak out of the school, but the jocks had found him, beaten him senseless, and sent him off to the hospital.

When he'd woken up, his father had been sitting at his beside with a grim expression on his face. His father had stared down at him for a long moment, then said, "Serves you right for being queer." Standing up, the man who had once given him piggybacks around the backyard while Ken shouted *giddy-up!* had walked out of the room and out of Ken's life.

When Ken was released from the hospital, he was sent to live with his grandmother in San Antonio. His father still wasn't talking to him and wouldn't until he "straightened up." His mother called him in secret and sometimes sent him gifts, but his childhood had ended at seventeen and so had his relationship with his parents.

"The 'one' ain't going to ditch you for some bitchy queen and run off to Canada and get married," Lenore chided him. She put one hand on her plump hip and glared at him. "You should know that by now. If they love you, they stay by you."

Ken wiped a tear away and some of his makeup came off with it. "I know! I know! But I gave up everything I had in Dallas to move here to be with him and he left me for some stupid peroxide blond with a fake orange tan!"

Lenore rolled her eyes. "He has bad taste."

"Hey!"

"I meant with whathisface. Not you. You're adorable."

"Really?"

Lenore frowned and said reluctantly, "Yes, for a melodramatic princess."

Ken gave her a pout, then shook his head. "I'm not melodramatic. He ripped my heart out. Tore it out and flung it away, then ran after it and stomped on it, then ground it into the dirt and..."

Mr. Cloy pushed open the door and peered in at them. "Y'all hear what's going on in Austin?"

Ken set his chin on his fist and shook his head. He tried to tone down his Nancy Boy inclinations when around the men in town. They were actually quite nice to him and one had even told him that "for a queer boy, you're okay." But he was also a businessman and he tried not to cause a stir among potential clients. There were enough stupid rumors about gay people in the world that he did not want anyone painting on him.

"Nope. What's up with Austin?"

"Got riots there, too. It's really getting crazy. It's like all the big cities are just going nuts," Mr. Cloy said, letting the door slam shut behind him. It was a heavy wood door with a leaded glass window set into it. Thick black velvet curtains with gold thread brocade covered the two big bay windows in the front of the store and kept out the hot sun.

Lenore broke down the box the hair extensions had come in and sighed. "Something bad going on. Maybe some bad crack or something."

Mr. Cloy scratched his chin. "It's on purpose. I know it. Someone has put something in the air or in the water. You know that old guy on public access is always going on about that stuff."

Ken knew exactly whom he was talking about. The geezer would come on public access once a week to ramble on about the government creating clones to do their dirty work. Back in the day, Darryl had watched it religiously. Of course, that was before Darryl hit his midlife crisis, sold the house without telling Ken, got himself a bimbo boyfriend, and hightailed it out of town leaving only a note on his pillow telling Ken he had to move out and that the shop was his.

"Well, I don't like the news. I don't like hearing sad stuff or scary stuff, but if something major is going down, I think it has to be those crazy Muslims," Ken decided. "Seriously, they hate us."

"Oh, Lord," Lenore drawled.

"They do! Because we're rich and stuff."

Lenore walked over and folded her arms across her ample bosom. "Okay, so they hate us. But why come and put a bunch of bad stuff in the water so we start eating each other and being all crazy?"

"Because they want to destroy us from within 'cause they hate our freedom," Mr. Cloy told her. "Honey, you're still young-"

"Do not honey me!" Lenore snapped. "I know what is going on just as much as you do and they hate us cause we're over there messing in their business."

"Look here, Missy Democrat," Ken said going all-Republican on her. "If they weren't messing in our business-"

"It is the responsibility of the United States of America as the only superpower in the world to police-" Mr. Cloy started up.

"Oh, and what about China?" Lenore cut in.

It was an old argument between the three of them. Ken was an old school Republican that still adored

Reagan. Mr. Cloy was a Neo-Conservative Republican that disagreed completely with Ken's sexual orientation, yet liked him anyway. Lenore was a hardcore Democrat. And all three loved to debate and argue. It was almost gleeful when they started up.

Ken was about to unleash his best speech on China when the sound of police sirens pierced their conversation. Mr. Cloy, who had been making a point about the moral superiority of the United States, stopped in mid-sentence.

A car outside slammed on its brakes and there was a loud screech as they locked. The terrifying sound of two large metal objects slamming together quickly followed.

"Shit," Mr. Cloy said, his eyes going wide behind his glasses.

Ken darted around the counter and whipped back one of the curtains. Outside were six cars: two smashed together, a van, a station wagon, and two police cruisers hemming them in. Steam was billowing out from under the crumpled hood of one of the crashed cars and people were pouring out of the vehicles. Some were shouting, others were crying. A few were covered in blood.

"Oh shit," Ken said.

Lenore took one long look at the scene. "It's here," she said simply.

3.
Things Going Bad Fast

Lenore took a long hard look at the chaos right outside their door. Two highway patrol cars and the town's only police car had the wreck surrounded. The people pouring out of the crashed vehicles were families with children, and the cops hesitated on drawing their weapons.

Mr. Cloy opened the door slightly so they could hear what was going on. Ken reached out and laid his hand on her shoulder. She knew the gesture was not only to comfort her, but also him. She rested her hand on his fingers and slightly squeezed.

"Please, we're just trying to get away!" A young white woman with brown hair sobbed uncontrollably, holding her baby tight. "Please! We have to get away from the highway!"

"Ma'am, calm down," one of the highway patrolmen said. His hand lingered near his weapon, but he looked calm. "You were going over a hundred miles per hour. That's not safe."

"It's not safe back there!" A Hispanic man spoke up, his face was bruised and blood was splattered over his shirt. His family was still in their vehicle. The mother leaned over the back of her seat trying to calm their children. "It's insane on the highway. We had to get off of it!"

"People were hurting each other...ripping each other apart...even...even..." another woman cried out.

"They were *eating* each other!" An older white man shouted out the dramatic words. His face was so red Lenore wondered if he was going to pop a blood vessel. "We got the hell out of the city when things started going bad, but out on the highway there was a car accident and it slowed all the traffic down. Next thing you know there are these...things...people...they were pulling people out of cars...and...eating them!" The man wiped his face with the back of his hand. "They pulled my wife out of the car...and I couldn't...I couldn't..." He began to sob and silence fell over the road.

The Hispanic man covered in bruises and blood continued the story. "We had to drive up the embankment to get off the highway. Then everyone started to try and do it! We were the first ones off, so we made it to the frontage and we just floored it!"

"Look, we're hearing about the violence in the cities and a thing or two about the car wrecks on the highways but that doesn't give you the right to speed down these roads. There are children, pets, old people-" one of the highway patrolman started to say.

"Then give us a ticket and we'll leave!" This was from the first woman clutching the baby. "We'll leave!"

The town's only policeman, Chief Murphy, pulled up on his belt and said in a soothing voice, "Okay, everyone just calm down. I know you folks saw something bad back there, but we need to keep this orderly."

"You have no idea what we saw back there!" one of the drivers shouted. "You have no idea."

Mr. Cloy leaned toward Lenore and Ken and whispered. "City folk always think they can just come out here and do what they want."

"Did you hear what they were saying?" Lenore asked him incredulously. Mr. Cloy had a one-track mind, but he was being ridiculous

Ken nodded in agreement. "I don't blame them for freaking out. What they said sounds crazy, but look at them! They're freaking traumatized."

Mr. Cloy frowned deeply, his hands in his jean pockets. "Say what you will, but this is the kinda thing that always turns out wrong. City people coming out here and making up their own rules and--"

"Carlos, help me!" A woman's shrill scream sent Lenore's skin crawling. "Something is wrong with the kids!"

A man rushed to open the door of one of the cars and the gathering crowd surged forward to see what was wrong. Mr. Cloy pushed the door to the shop all the way open and the three of them took several steps outside to see what was going on.

The highway patrolmen hurried forward and told everyone to step back as the Sheriff helped the distressed parents lift one of their kids out of the back of the car. It was a teenage girl and she was having an appalling seizure. Blood gushed from a wound in her neck. A second child stumbled out of the car, clutching at the older girl. As everyone watched in terror, he leaned down and took a large bite of flesh from her forearm.

"Ramon, no!" His mother grabbed the boy and wrestled him from his sister.

"Oh, shit!" Ken seized Lenore's arm and squeezed. "Did that just happen? Did that just happen?"

Lenore felt queasy. "Uh huh, that baby just went crazy and tried to eat his sister."

The highway patrolmen pushed the gawking spectators back, then turned their attention to the girl on the ground. Her father was cradling her in his arms and sobbing. Meanwhile, the little boy who had taken a hunk out of his sister was chewing as his mother and several other people tried to drag him a safe distance away.

"Get it out of his mouth!" his mother screamed.

One of the people trying to help her reached toward the boy's mouth.

"This is gonna get bad fast," Lenore said in a low voice.

"Uh huh," Ken agreed.

Together, they started backing toward the door to the beauty shop.

4.
Things Getting Worse Faster

Ken's grip on Lenore's hand tightened as they backed toward the open doorway of the beauty shop.

"Hey, don't touch that kid," Mr. Cloy called out, stepping into the street.

The man reaching out to pull the chunk of flesh from the child's bloodied mouth hesitated. The kid swallowed what he was eating and lunged forward. The man and the mother of the child screamed as the kid's hard teeth clamped on the fingers paused before his face.

At the same time, the teenage girl on the ground stopped convulsing and her father let out an anguished cry. He attempted to throw himself over her, but one of the highway patrolmen shoved him back.

"Hold on! Let us work on her," the patrolman said in an authoritative tone.

Screams and shouts filled the morning air as one group of people tried to wrestle the child off the screaming man while the other group gathered around the girl lying bloodied and dead on the road.

"Get inside, get inside!" Ken whispered urgently to Lenore.

"I ain't arguing."

They both slipped into the shop, shut the door, and stared through the thick glass.

Mr. Cloy hovered near the edge of the crowd watching with a shocked look on his face.

"Why doesn't that damn fool get inside?" Lenore muttered.

"Why don't any of them?" Ken clutched her arm tightly. "This is not good! So not good!"

A tug of war continued as the mother pulled on her child and two men pulled on his victim. The boy's hard little teeth rent most of the skin off the two fingers as they were ripped from his mouth.

Clutching his bloodied hand, the man howled in pain. He ran along the street with several of his friends behind him.

"Oh, crap," Ken exclaimed as the kid wiggled around in his mother's grasp and tore into her chest.

"Okay, Damian needs to be put down," Lenore decided firmly.

The boy's seemingly-dead sister sat up and people applauded with relief even though ten feet away the other child was taking huge bites out of his mother. The insanity of the moment made Ken's head hurt. People were just not getting what was going on. Hell, he wasn't sure what was going on.

The highway patrolman motioned everyone back and turned to the resurrected teenager. The father of the girl again tried to reach for her, but was pushed away.

"Sir, just step back. We got an ambulance on the way," he told the father a soothing tone. Kneeling down, he gazed into the blank face of the teenager. "Miss, you're going to be all right."

People clapped again as she gripped him by the neck. It was obvious they thought she was going to hug or kiss her rescuer. Lenore grabbed Ken's arm as the girl opened her mouth wide and drove her teeth into the officer's face.

"And now we've got Carrie!" Ken couldn't believe what he was seeing.

At long last, the crowd of people, from both the cars and the town, comprehended the true danger of the situation. The girl pinned the patrolman to the ground and ripped huge bites of skin from his face and neck. The second patrolman drew his gun, flicked off the safety and pulled the trigger. The bullets punched through the girl's body and into the patrolman beneath her.

Her father wailed in despair as he spun around in a circle, becoming aware that all his family had become monsters. The older man grabbed the father's arm and shoved him into a car.

"We need to go!" the older man shouted.

Much to Ken's relief, the woman with the baby crawled into the van as the rest of the highway refugees piled into their vehicles.

Nearby two men managed to get the boy off his mother and she collapsed to the ground, her neck spurting long fountains of blood. The boy thrashed between the two men. The men seemed at a loss as to what to do now that they had him off the mother.

The dead girl sluggishly stood up and lurched toward the remaining patrolman. He finished reloading and began firing at her again.

"Get out of here!" Sheriff Murphy shouted at the last of the shocked bystanders.

People sprinted away as the cars performed a crazy dance, attempting to maneuver out from between the highway patrol cars and escape.

"This can't get worse," Ken said in a soft voice.

Mr. Cloy finally seemed to register that he was in danger and retreated toward his store. A van, full of panicked people, crashed into the side of one of the patrol cars as it tried to skirt around it.

Sheriff Murphy ran toward the van, attempting to wave to the driver, but the vehicle reversed and lurched forward again. It struck the Sheriff. The older man's body was thrown by the impact and skidded to a stop near Ken's shop. The driver of the van didn't even seem to realize what he had done as he crashed his vehicle into the patrol car again, finally scooting it out of the way.

"Oh, no, honey. It's worse," Lenore said in a trembling voice.

The zombie girl leaped onto the lawman shooting at her. The patrolman she had been chewing on minutes before rose to his feet and let out an ungodly screech.

The two townspeople struggling with the little boy seemed to finally get a plan together and swung him back and forth between them, gaining momentum before releasing him. The kid arced through the air and smashed into a departing car. The two men then turned to run. One of them let out a yelp as the boy's mother dragged him down to the ground. She did not hesitate in biting into his arm.

The bloodied and torn undead patrolman let out another ungodly howl and ran after the last man trying to dodge the departing cars and escape. The van that had run down Sheriff Murphy disappeared from view and the other cars followed.

"Where's that demented little freak?" Lenore asked anxiously.

"There." Ken pointed to the boy as he limped on an broken leg toward Sheriff Murphy. A bone was sticking out of his thigh, but the kid moved with determination toward the fallen lawman.

"Do something!"

"Like what? Go tell him he's bad and put him in the corner?" Ken looked around at his shop, unable to even comprehend what he could use to stop the little boy.

Lenore grabbed the coat rack next to the door, yanked the door open, and charged out. Ken gasped, but shadowed after her. Lenore rushed to the Sheriff's side and swung the coat rack, knocking the zombie kid off his feet. The kid hissed, trying to get up, but Lenore smacked him again.

"You lil' bastard, stay down!"

Ken took hold of the Sheriff's arms and started to drag him back to the shop. It was difficult, but he was physically fit from his daily workout and managed to get the bigger man up over the curb.

Close by, the teenage girl was pulling the intestines out of the screaming patrolman while his former partner ran down the man who had tried to save the mother. The zombie tackled the man to the ground and ripped into him with his teeth. Meanwhile, the mother was still attacking the second man who had tried to help her.

Lenore smacked the kid off his feet again as she shifted backward toward the shop. "Get the Sheriff inside."

"Almost there," Ken huffed, dragging the Sheriff into the entrance.

The kid climbed to his feet and charged Lenore. Again, she used the coat rack to knock him on his ass. This time she continued to smack him with the rack, trying to keep him down.

Beyond Lenore, the mother was done eating. She climbed to her feet as her victim crawled to his knees behind her and let out a terrible moan of hunger.

"Hurry up, Lenore," Ken shouted at her. "I got him inside!"

Lenore gave the kid one more big push, then ran to the shop.

Ken felt his throat tighten as the two mangled adults and the demonic child charged after her.

"Lenore, run! Run!"

Lenore was amazingly fast despite her size and hurled into the beauty shop. Ken slammed the door and moved to lock it.

"The keys!"

Lenore looked at him quizzically as she set the coatrack back in place, then understood. "Oh!" She stumbled over the Sheriff as she moved to snag the keys from the cash register.

Ken looked up to see the three crazed cannibals rushing toward the door. He quickly pulled the shade down over the window.

"Like that'll work," he muttered, then looked toward Lenore. "Keys would be, like, so good right now."

"Hold on, looking for them. You always put them in the wrong place," Lenore answered as she rummaged through the drawer under the register.

"Okay, like now, you know, would be good." Ken held out his hand. He let out a girly yelp as something hit the door on the other side. He shot a look at the doorknob and felt his heart began to beat even faster.

"Catch!"

Ken glanced up just in time to see the ring of keys flying at his head. For a moment, he thought he wasn't going to catch them, then his fingers caught the miniature Barbie doll dangling from the ring. He quickly inserted the key with the big pink heart on it into the lock as the door vibrated under the assault of the people on the other side. The doorknob jiggled and Ken had to fight to twist the key in the lock. Finally, the big bolts slid into place and Ken backed away from the door.

Lenore stepped next to him and they both stared at the door.

"Will it hold?"

"It's a hundred years old and like petrified wood," Ken answered.

"But will it hold?"

"Um..."

They both stared at the quivering door as the Sheriff moaned softly at their feet.

5.
It Gets Even Worse

"Okay...so..." Ken waved toward the door. "They're like...um..."

"Zombies," Lenore said.

"Yeah. That." Ken frowned deeply. "Which means I'm either drunk, high, insane or-"

"-the dead people decided we're good eatin'."

"Right." Ken arched an eyebrow. "Great."

Lenore frowned even more deeply than usual before motioning to the big antique wardrobe that served as storage for hair dyes. "I think we should move that in front of the door."

Ken eyed the Sheriff warily. "What about him?"

"First things first," Lenore answered, heading over to the wardrobe.

Ken scurried into the back storage room that doubled as his office to retrieve the dolley.

Lenore gave the trembling shop door a dark look before tossing all the bottles of dyes and creams onto the nearby sofa. She wasn't too worried about the bottles breaking since she figured the dead getting up and eating people was much more important than fighting with the supplier over the availability of certain colors. Behind her the Sheriff moaned, but didn't stir. Of course, that wasn't half as worrisome as the growls just outside the front door.

Ken rushed back with the dolley and together they wrestled the big piece of furniture in front of the door. There was much cursing and general swearing, but they managed to get the wardrobe positioned. Pushing it flush against it was difficult though.

"Push harder," Ken ordered her.

"You push harder, skinny boy," she grumbled. It was unnerving to even be near the shaking door and hear the moans and screeches from the other side.

The heavy oak wardrobe finally slid into place and they both stepped back to survey their work.

"Well," Ken said, "that really doesn't make me feel safer."

"Not with those two big freaking windows behind the curtains," Lenore agreed.

"Let's put stuff in front of the curtains to slow them down if the get in," Ken suggested.

Together they dragged every heavy piece of furniture in the shop over to the windows to build a wall up behind the curtains. They were too afraid to actually move the curtains and press the furniture up against the glass. They noticed the zombies were actually quieter now that they couldn't see the humans inside the shop.

"Think they gotta see us to get riled up," Lenore wondered aloud.

"Or maybe they're eating someone out there," Ken offered.

"And you say I'm doom and gloom." Lenore put her hands on her hips and surveyed their handiwork. "Might slow 'em down."

Again, the Sheriff moaned behind them.

"We really should see if we can help him and maybe call 911," Ken decided. He knelt next to the older man and gaped at him fearfully. "His breathing sounds really bad."

"I think his lungs are filling with blood," Lenore answered, moving toward the phone.

"You took medical training?"

"No. I watch *House*." Lenore picked up the phone and punched in her grandmother's phone number. As she expected, the line was busy. "World is coming to an end and she's gossiping about her soap opera." With a sigh, Lenore dialed 911 and held out the phone so Ken could hear the busy signal.

"This is not happening!" Ken exclaimed. "Seriously, I'm asleep and this is not a good dream. I would much rather have Daniel Craig as James Bond whisking me off to the French Rivera."

Lenore rolled her eyes, walked over and pinched Ken as hard as she could.

"Bitch!"

"You're not sleeping or dreaming," Lenore said firmly. She could feel her brow puckering as she frowned. Regardless of all her grandmother's warnings about frown lines she didn't really care right now. She was annoyed to no end that the world had decided to go to hell today. It was damn inconvenient and she really didn't want to deal with it. But, of course, she would.

"Let's drag him out the back door and take him to the hospital," she said finally.

"Okay, but should we move him?"

"You already moved him once. If that didn't make it worse, this probably won't either." Lenore sighed wearily. "Let's do it. We'll get him to the car, go get my grandma, and head to the hospital." She was worried about her grandmother and the Sheriff was looking pretty bad. Ken was keeping it together a bit better than she'd expected, but she knew they were both probably in some sort of weird shock.

The pounding on the front door was reduced to what sounded like small fists now. Probably the evil zombie kid. Lenore carefully split the curtain near her with her finger and peeked out.

The little kid was still pounding on the door, but the adults were not in sight. The street appeared empty. The puddles of blood and bits of flesh strewn about the haphazardly-parked police cars made Lenore's stomach clench. She slid her gaze to the little one banging on the door. He was snarling and hissing and she had the desire to slap him silly. Of course, he'd only try to eat her.

Dropping the curtain into place, Lenore said to Ken, "We just got the little kid outside the door."

"Where are the rest?" Ken lightly patted the Sheriff's hand. It was obvious he didn't know what else to do.

"Beats me. Trying to eat someone else, probably."

The phone suddenly rang beside her and, in spite of her determination to keep calm, she jerked in surprise. She snatched up the phone and said, "Hello?" She hoped to hear her grandmother's voice.

"Lenore," Mr. Cloy's voice whispered. "They're trying to get in my store."

"Did you call the police?"

"You mean the guy lying on the floor in your shop?" Mr. Cloy sounded both afraid and peeved.

"Good point. Where you at?"

"Hiding behind the counter hoping if they can't see me they'll lose interest."

"You got a weapon?"

There was a long moment of silence, then Mr. Cloy said, "I left it in my truck. I took it home to clean and take to the range and I forgot it in my truck."

Lenore frowned and leaned against the counter. "Okay, we're about to leave with the Sheriff for the hospital. Can you sneak to the back of the store and be ready to leave by the alley door?"

"There are cracks in the window," Mr. Cloy said in a trembling voice.

"Are you listening to me? Can you move to the back of the store?"

"I'm afraid to move. They're trying so hard to get in. What if they see me and it makes them even crazier? I really thought the rapture would happen by this point. I really did." He sounded close to hysteria.

"Okay, we will honk when we are behind your store. That is when you get up, run to the door, open it and get to the car. Okay?"

There was a sharp intake of breath. "Okay."

"Then we gotta plan. See you in a few."

Lenore hung up and grumbled to herself. She walked to the back of the store and grabbed Ken's rolling office chair. Mumbling the whole time about zombies and people freaking out, she dragged it to the Sheriff and Ken.

Ken was very quiet as he fearfully stared at the old man.

"Help me get him up," Lenore ordered.

"He's dead," Ken answered softly.

"What?"

"He just kinda let out this long breath then stopped breathing. I checked his pulse." Ken wiped a tear away from his cheek.

"You better step back in case he gets up," Lenore urged.

Ken crawled backward, his body trembling. He rested his back against the wall and stared at the old man blankly. "Lenore, I couldn't do anything."

"It's not your fault," Lenore said firmly.

"Is he gonna come back?"

"I don't know," Lenore answered. She grabbed the coat rack and stood over the old man. "I guess we'll find out."

In silence, they waited.

6.
Where To Go?

Lenore split her attention between the body and the clock on the wall. The coat rack was increasingly heavier, but she had to be ready if the Sheriff did decide to sit up and eat them. Ken plucked a heavy lamp off a table, ditched the lampshade, and wound the cord around the base. It was a good bludgeoning weapon.

"If he gets up, I'll hit him first then you," Lenore instructed Ken.

"I'm ready." Ken hoisted the lamp stand over his head. He appeared both scared and determined.

Five minutes passed.

"He's not getting up," Ken said at last.

"Yeah, I think you're right."

"The ones outside got up right away."

Lenore poked at the body with the coat rack. There was no response. "Well, zombies aren't smart enough to fake it."

"I think he's really, really dead." Ken poked the Sheriff's head a few times with his foot. It lolled about a little, but the Sheriff did not move otherwise. "Yep. Dead."

"Okay. Then we leave now and get Mr. Cloy," Lenore decided.

"I'm so ready to not be here with dead things." Ken headed to the rear of the store. Lenore trudged along behind him.

"Got your keys?"

Ken frowned. "Of course-oh, wait!" He dashed to the counter, giving wide berth to the dead body on the floor, and grabbed up his keys from beside the cash register. "What would I do without you?"

"Let's not find out," Lenore answered.

Ken rushed to her side and together they stared at the heavy wood door that opened onto the alley. "I'm scared."

"Me, too."

"I never watched horror movies growing up. They scared me too much. I'm not ready for this," Ken said in a trembling voice. He wrapped his arms around her and laid his head on her shoulder.

Reaching up, Lenore patted his hair, stiff with hair gel and hairspray, and sighed. "Me neither. I thought they were stupid movies."

"So neither one of us knows what we're doing," Ken groaned.

"Yep. But then again, it's a unique situation. It's not like dead babies get up every day and start eating everyone."

"Unless you live in L.A." Ken was convinced everything bad on the planet originated in L.A.

Lenore rolled her eyes and heaved the coat rack over her shoulder. "Okay, open the door."

"I really don't wanna."

"Dead body behind us," she reminded him.

"Fine!"

Ken whipped open the door. The alley came into view. Ken's small Volkswagen convertible was parked just across from the back door under a carport. Between the door and the Volkswagen were five zombies greedily ripping apart some poor person and stuffing bits of flesh and gore into their mouths.

"Shut the door," Lenore ordered.

Ken stared in horror. "I think they're eating the mailman."

Lenore reached out and slammed the door shut just as the zombies realized there were fresh humans standing nearby. Sliding the heavy bolts into place and twirling the deadbolts until they locked, Lenore felt her stomach heaving. Beside her, Ken sobbed softly. Something hit the door on the other side and faintly they could hear the dead thing growling.

Overcome, Lenore stumbled to a nearby sink they used for cleaning up the brushes and bowls and threw up. Tears stung her eyes as her stomach kept emptying and her body was wracked with tremors. Ken's hands delicately pulled her hair back and he stood next to her until she finished. She rinsed her mouth out with water as Ken rubbed her back and whispered that it would be okay.

Slowly straightening, she tried not to let him see she was crying. "Mr. Cloy is in danger. We were supposed to pick him up. They're trying to get into his store."

Behind them, the banging on the back door continued.

"We can't go out through the alley. Can we go out the front? Maybe whack the little demon kid?"

"The other ones are right next door. If we go out and they rush us..." Lenore shook her head. "We're kinda stuck."

Ken suddenly looked excited. "The gun! The gun! The Sheriff has a gun!"

Together they raced over to the man's body and knelt beside it. They both reached for the holster at the same time only to realize it was empty.

"What the hell?" Ken looked around the store.

"I got a bad feeling," Lenore said, heaving herself to her feet. She moved over to the window and cracked the curtain just a little.

The little bastard was still pounding on the door, but didn't notice her. In the street more of the dead things wandered around. They were fairly messed up and it was hard to tell if they were townspeople or not, though a few looked slightly familiar. She scanned the street and sighed.

"Gun is out in the street. He must have had it in his hand."

She let the curtain fall into place.

The phone began to ring again. Ken snatched it up. "Hello? Mr. Cloy? Yes. We were going to get you but there are more zombies in the alley. Um. Um. You don't have an office in the back you can lock yourself in? Well, true. You'd be trapped with no exit. Uh."

Lenore grabbed the phone from Ken. "Go up to your storage room and lock yourself in. At least you got a window up there. Yeah, I know it has bars. But you're in a hardware store. Grab something-"

Even in the beauty shop they heard the glass shatter next door. It was a frightful sound and Lenore heard Mr. Cloy gasp in terror.

"Run to the storage room upstairs!"

The phone on the other end hit the floor and she heard footsteps rushing away from it as the moans and screeches of the dead grew louder.

She banged the phone down.

Through the thick brick walls, they heard the cries of the dead.

"I want to go upstairs," Ken said finally.

Lenore jumped at the sound of someone thumping their fists against the beauty shop window started. "Yeah. I think you're right. They're all stirred up now."

Together they hurried to the door to the stairwell that led to the second floor. Ken quickly unlocked it and they both stepped inside. Ken twirled the deadbolts into place.

They rushed up the long wooden staircase to the floor above.

"I hate today," Ken said.

"I'm there with you," Lenore agreed.

Unlocking the door to his apartment, Ken said, "We need to get a plan together. Stat."

Lenore stopped on the step below him and took a deep breath. "Right now, I just wanna sit down for a minute and not think about it."

Ken nodded and opened the door to his apartment.

Next door, they could hear Mr. Cloy screaming their names.

7.
The Fate of Mr. Cloy

The morning sun poured through the high windows of Ken's apartment, filling the stylishly-decorated space with glorious light that illuminated the leather furniture and the art nouveau paintings that hung in antique frames on the walls. It was a perfect setting, except for Mr. Cloy's voice screaming their names next door.

Ken drew in a few deep breaths and prayed to God it would be over soon. How long would it take for the zombies to kill Mr. Cloy? He felt tears sliding down his cheeks as the screaming continued. Next to him, Lenore sank down into a chair and put her face in her hands.

Together, they waited for the feeding frenzy to be over and prayed for Mr. Cloy's screams to end.

Shaking, Ken sat down on the sofa and began to rearrange the fresh flowers in the china bowl on the coffee table. He couldn't think of anything else to do and he just couldn't sit still.

The screaming didn't stop.

"Why won't it end?" Lenore finally said.

Ken blinked, then whispered, "Oh, shit." He realized Mr. Cloy wasn't screaming because he was being eaten. He was screaming to get their attention.

Jumping to his feet, Ken indicated for Lenore to follow him to the room next to the front door. It was a room that he had yet to renovate. The roof had leaked and the wood was rotted and the walls moldy. The estimate on how much it would cost to renovate had been out of his price range so he had shut the door and pretended the room didn't exist.

"The foundation settled a few years ago after a bad serics of storms and the wall in here pulled away from the main part of the building. This section was an add-on." Ken explained as he unlocked the door and shoved it open. "It used to be an open porch. Mr. Cloy's building was built after this one and was built right up against it.

A tornado during that big storm tore the second floor off of Mr. Cloy's building except for the old storage room. They never rebuilt the second floor. They just fixed up what they could. I think I know what he's doing."

"Thanks for the history lesson, but show me what the hell is going on," Lenore snapped.

Ken pointed to a corner that was flush to Mr. Cloy's building. There was yellowed caulk bubbling out of the crevice. "There is a crack in the wall that goes through to the storage room. My bastard ex put caulk here as a temporary fix." The crack was almost two inches wide.

Mr. Cloy was still screaming their names.

"I think I gotcha," Lenore said.

Together, they began to pull at the hard and dirty caulk with their fingers, then resorted to chipping it out with knives Ken retrieved from the kitchen. It took some hard work, but they finally got a section cleared out.

Pressing firmly against the wall, Ken could peer through the crack to the other side. Mr. Cloy's eye was staring right back at him.

"Took you long enough," Mr. Cloy's lips said under his big bushy black mustache.

"We thought you were getting eaten," Ken explained.

"They're in the store, but I got two doors between them and me right now," Mr. Cloy answered.

Lenore shoved Ken out of the way and said, "You got stuff to make this wider?"

"I don't keep anything up here. You got something on your side?"

Lenore snorted. "Ken's idea of tools is a knife for a screwdriver and a heel of his boots for a hammer."

"Hey," Ken protested, though it was true.

"It would take forever anyway. Got at least two feet of quarry rock and mortar between us. I'm gonna try and pry the bars off the window. The tornado did a lot of damage and they're kinda loose already. If I can get onto the roof of the storage room, maybe you guys can haul me up onto the roof of your building. There ain't no windows facing my way on your second floor."

"Okay, let us know when you're ready. That sounds like a decent enough plan. They ain't in our building yet." Lenore stepped away from the wall and gave Ken an annoyed look. "You do have rope, right?"

Ken hesitated then said meekly, "No. But we can tie sheets together."

Lenore rolled her eyes and Ken ignored her to flatten himself against the wall to see Mr. Cloy one more time. "We'll get you over here then make plans. We can do this!"

Mr. Cloy's laughter was a welcome sound. "With you and Lenore on my side, I feel safe as a baby at his mama's teat."

"Ew," Ken answered. "Baby slobber."

This made Mr. Cloy laugh again as Ken saw him pull away from the crack to start work on the window. It sucked that they didn't have a way to bash through the wall, but then again, if they made a hole in the wall and the dead guys got into the storage room...yep, it was better to haul him up onto the roof.

Ken left the room and found Lenore standing in his kitchen, calling her grandmother again. From the look on her face, he knew she had a busy signal again. It wasn't uncommon for her grandmother to be on the phone chatting, but on a day like today, it was more than annoying.

Lenore clutched the phone tightly in her hand, then forced herself to set it down lightly. "She's not answering."

"Let's get the rope ready," Ken said in a voice he hoped sounded both soothing and strong.

With a curt nod, Lenore followed him to the linen closet. His silk and satin sheets were dismissed quickly. They would be far too slippery, but the new cotton sheets he had bought would suffice. It hurt to cut the 800 thread count sheets into long, wide strips, but at least they would be velvety soft against Mr. Cloy's hands when he climbed onto their roof.

"You better not tear up over these sheets," Lenore muttered at him.

"But they're Egyptian cotton," Ken sniffled.

"I'm so gonna punch you."

They knotted the ends together and tested them by pulling as hard they could. Lenore solidly won the tug of war. Ken ended up in her arms and gave her his most demure smile. She rolled her eyes and tugged the makeshift rope out of his hands.

"I'll go check on him." Ken skipped back to the room before she could let him have it. He loved teasing Lenore. It was more fun than he cared to admit. Though she would grumpily respond, he could tell she liked it as much as he did. He pressed himself against the wall and shouted into the crack.

"Hey, Mr. Cloy!"

It took a moment, but Mr. Cloy's eye and bushy mustache came into view beyond the narrow fissure in the wall. "They're up to the second door now."

Ken inhaled sharply and listened for a moment. What he had thought was Mr. Cloy trying to get a bar out of the window was the dead actually beating on the door. "Oh, shit. Are you ready?"

"Almost got the second one out. I should be able to crawl out after that. Give me five minutes."

"Do you have five minutes?"

"Dunno. Done wasting time. See you up top," Mr. Cloy answered, then vanished from view.

Trying not to wring his hands or run like a Nancy boy, Ken dashed out into the living room, feeling panic welling up inside of him. "They're about to bust into the storage room. We need to get up on top!"

"Aw, shit. I hate today."

Together they climbed the narrow staircase to the roof. Lenore muttered about it being too narrow, but Ken shushed her. He could feel his nerves getting the best of him and his hands were shaking. The old stairway was supposed to be for maintenance and it was musty and dusty. He never used it and he felt embarrassed with his lack of housekeeping. They reached the roof and he shoved open the door.

The small town swam into view and he felt overwhelmed by the bright, glaring sunlight. He shaded his eyes. What looked like a quiet serene Texas town at first blush soon revealed itself to be a place of death and destruction. A building was burning on the edge of town and in the streets people were running, screaming, and attacking each other. Car crashes littered intersections and somewhere nearby a woman was screaming.

It was hell.

"I really hate today," Lenore muttered.

Together they hurried to the edge of the building and peered down at the small storage room that lay flush against Ken's building. There was no sign of Mr. Cloy.

"Mr. Cloy! Mr. Cloy!" Their voices were a chorus and Ken noted his voice sounded quite high next to Lenore's. His stomach churned and he felt his hands shaking as he gripped the edge of the building.

Mr. Cloy finally appeared and struggled to worm his way out of the window. The fit was tight.

"C'mon, Mr. Cloy!" They both started shouting encouragement and waving at him as if it would somehow help.

Mr. Cloy's face tilted upward and they saw he had a look of pure terror on his face. That one look said it all. The zombies were about to break into the storage room. Gripping the wall, Mr. Cloy tried desperately to slide through the bars. His stomach finally squeezed through and he fell onto the roof.

"Hurry, hurry!" Ken's voice reflected his fear and he swallowed hard to avoid vomiting.

Lenore had already secured the rope around a pipe sticking out of roof, and she tossed the line down to Mr. Cloy. He reached out with eager hands to grasp it.

Behind him, battered hands and twisted, bloodied faces appeared in the window.

Wrapping the makeshift rope around his wrist, Mr. Cloy said, "Pull me up!"

Ken and Lenore heaved him up. Mr. Cloy was surprisingly heavy in spite of his skinny frame. The muscles in Ken's arms and shoulders strained with the weight. Abruptly the rope went slack and Ken and Lenore both fell to the roof.

Shocked, they scrambled to their feet and looked over the edge of the roof to see Mr. Cloy lying on top of the storage room. Breathing heavily, he gave them a small wave.

"I can't join you, kids," Mr. Cloy said in a ragged voice as he tried to catch his breath. He pointed toward his leg, then lifted his pant cuff.

"Oh, shit," Lenore whispered.

Fresh tears sprung to Ken's eyes as huge gouges in Mr. Cloy's flesh were revealed.

"They got me when I was coming out the window," Mr. Cloy sobbed. "It's the bite that does it."

Ken shivered. The bloodied, feral faces in the window groaned. The dead creatures stretched grasping hands in his direction, their milky eyes glowering up at him and Lenore.

No one spoke as the moans and howls the dead filled the air.

8.
At Hell's Mouth

"This is bullshit," Ken declared.

Lenore shushed him as he stomped his foot and crossed his arms in irritation.

They stood at the edge of the building watching Mr. Cloy. Their friend and neighbor sat in silence, arms resting on his knees and his head bowed. Beneath him, the zombies clawed at the bars and edges of the window.

The heat of the sun weighed down on Ken's shoulders and made them itch. Perspiration slid down his spine. He frowned. He hated being sweaty and hot, but he didn't want to leave Mr. Cloy to face his fate alone.

"We can't just leave him down there," Ken whispered to Lenore.

"We can try and make him comfortable. It's freaking hot out here," Lenore admitted. "Go get him stuff. I'm going to stay here with him."

Ken hurried downstairs and threw together items to make Mr. Cloy more comfortable. The air mattress and its pump were the first things he pulled out of his closet. He added an umbrella and a small fan that ran on batteries. Clean cotton sheets were added to the pile along with a pillow. In the kitchen, he tossed several water bottles and some cookies and chips into a tote bag. Finally, he lugged the whole thing upstairs, nearly tripping a few times, but managing to reach the top without falling down the stairs.

Lenore sat on the edge of the building staring out over the town. Ken nearly fell to his knees by the time he reached her with his load.

"He's not talking," she whispered to Ken.

"Well, he's, like, going to die and be one of those things," Ken said in a low voice back to her. "How would you feel?"

"I can hear you," Mr. Cloy said, slowly raising his head. He looked pale and was crying. "You ain't gotta whisper."

"I brought you stuff!" Ken heaved the duffel bag with the air mattress and bedding over the side of the building and dropped it down next to Mr. Cloy.

Mr. Cloy got to his feet and Ken lowered the rest of the stuff into his friend's waiting arms. Mr. Cloy sighed and held the bag close to his chest. "Thanks, Ken. I do appreciate this."

Lenore sat in silence and viewed the chaos happening in their small town. Her expression was inscrutable. Ken sat next to her and didn't say a word.

Mr. Cloy set up the air mattress and propped the umbrella so he could hide under its shade. He sat eating cookies as the dead moaned beneath his shelter.

Ken tried not to watch what was going on in the town, but he couldn't help it. Cars raced around with small packs of bloodied people chasing them. A few houses were under siege with the walking dead beating on the doors and windows. Gunshots barked in the distance and Ken heard a chainsaw start somewhere nearby.

"You guys don't have to stay out here with me," Mr. Cloy said finally. "I know you guys did your best by me, but I gotta face the Maker on my own now. I'm just...I just thought the rapture would come before now."

"Maybe this isn't the Tribulation," Ken suggested.

"I dunno. Dead coming out of their graves is somewhere in Revelations." Mr. Cloy's dark hair was glistening with sweat and he kept rubbing his bushy mustache.

"Well, it don't matter if it is or not. It's just a bad day all around," Lenore decided somberly.

Somewhere nearby, a baby was crying piteously.

"Yeah," Mr. Cloy said.

"Mr. Cloy-"

"Leslie," Mr. Cloy corrected Ken. "My name is Leslie."

"Really?" Ken raised an eyebrow.

"That's why I never use it. Sometimes go by Les, but then people said I was "less-than" and it just got to be an old joke." He shrugged. "I never gave you shit about being queer 'cause I got it enough when I was a kid 'cause of my name."

"Oh." Ken wasn't sure how to take that revelation.

Leslie Cloy, owner of Cloy's Hardware, surveyed the small town and wiped a tear away. "It don't matter no more, I guess, everything that happened before. The divorce from Bertha...the kids going to live in California with her. It's all done now. And this is the end. I don't feel I've done much with my life and it's not a good feeling. Always waiting for something to happen."

In the distance, the baby gave three sharp screams, then was silent. Lenore lowered her head. Ken felt his stomach heave, but he managed to keep his breakfast down.

"Nothing matters when it's all going to hell and there ain't nothing we can do," Mr. Cloy said and shook his head sadly.

"I ain't giving up," Lenore declared in a low, firm voice. "I'm not gonna just sit here and watch the world end and not do a damn thing to survive." She exhaled slowly. "I'm gonna go get my grandma."

"How?" Ken's voice sounded high-pitched even to him. Despite the chaos in the town around them, he felt safe perched high up on his building. The thought of going down into the hell in the streets below made his insides twitch.

"I don't know, but I'm going. I'm not giving up." Her voice was firm.

Mr. Leslie Cloy swallowed more water and ate another cookie. "Well, ain't much I can do no more."

Ken wanted to assure his old companion it would all be okay in the end, but he couldn't. Mr. Cloy would be one of the dead soon. They all knew they were on his deathwatch.

"You know what? I ain't going to sit here like a big ol' 'less-than.' I am on my way to meet my Maker, but you kids should at least get a shot at making it." Mr. Cloy stood and rummaged in his jean pocket before pulling out his truck keys. "Take my truck and get the hell out of here. My shotgun is in the rack. Shotgun shells are in the glove compartment."

He tossed the keys toward them and Lenore snatched them out of the air.

"That's like a really sweet offer, Mr. Cloy, but we really have a serious problem with dead things being in the street. It would be pretty hard to get to the truck," Ken reminded him.

Mr. Cloy nodded somberly, then shrugged. "It was a thought. Wait! I can distract them!"

"I so don't like the sound of that," Ken decided.

"I can go to the edge of the roof and see if maybe the ones in the street will respond to me yelling down at them. Then you guys can go out the front door of the shop and get to the truck. Maybe I can get them around to the side of the building." Mr. Cloy glanced at the desperate dead hands scrabbling at the sides of the window below. "They seem pretty determined to get to their prey once they got their sights on it. Gimme that rope."

Lenore shrugged at Ken and went to retrieve their makeshift rope.

"You're a good guy, Mr. Cloy," Ken said finally. "Seriously, an all-around good guy. You've always been super cool with me even when I knew you weren't all that comfortable with me being-"

"It ain't nothing. We're human beings. Gotta remember that. 'sides, Jesus never said nothin' about gay people, so I don't take what Pastor Baird said as gospel truth no how. You're okay in my book. Always were."

Lenore tossed the rope down to Mr. Cloy. He snagged it and promptly started tying it to a pipe sticking out of the top of the roof of the storage room.

"I'm gonna give it a trial shot and let you know how it goes," he called out.

"Thanks, Mr. Cloy-Leslie!" Ken felt tears in his eyes again and they burned almost as fiercely as the Texas sun.

With a nod, Mr. Cloy lowered himself off the storage room and limped across the roof of his building. The zombies in the storage room began to howl as they caught sight of him.

9.
Escape

Lenore stood with her arms folded over her ample bosom and once more swore to herself that she was not going to die today. There was no way on God's slowly-dying earth that she was going to give up and die. She didn't care how bad things looked, she didn't care how much the zombies howled, she didn't care about the fire in the distance, because she was not going to die today and that was that.

Through narrowed eyes she watched Mr. Cloy hobble toward the edge of his building. Behind him, the dead gathered in the small window of the storage room moaned for his flesh. It was a terrible sound that made her skin crawl. Coupled with the fierce heat of the sun beating down on her bare head, she was getting a terrible headache that was making her even crankier.

Beside her Ken was trembling. She could tell her buddy was trying to be brave, but his hands were quivering at his sides and she could see tears in his eyes. Ken was a sensitive soul even if he was a smart ass. She has half inclined to hug him and reassure him that everything was going to be okay, but they were both sweating like pigs and she really didn't like touching anyone anyway. She just wasn't very good with the whole touchy feely thing.

Mr. Cloy made it to the edge of the building and stayed for a long moment just staring down. Lenore figured he was trying to get up his nerve, but when he looked over his shoulder at them she could see his eyes were wide with fear.

"There are so many," he called out to them.

A fresh set of chills flowed down her spine.

Ken grabbed her hand and she gave it a hard squeeze. His skin was slick with sweat and she knew it was from more than the sun's fierce heat. Mr. Cloy looked terrified as he studied the street below. Lenore could see his knees knocking together and his jaw quivering. She wasn't sure if it was the infection or if it was the sight of what was below. Maybe it was a little of both.

"Okay, they are coming to..." Mr. Cloy wiped sweat from the back of his neck. "They're all gathering down below me. I think...I think maybe I can hold them here so you guys can sneak out and get to my truck."

"Do you think we should risk it?" Ken's voice was raw with fear.

"Yeah. Cause I ain't staying here to get trapped by those things," Lenore answered firmly. "I'm going. If you want to stay, you can, Ken, but I don't think it will be such a good idea."

Ken chewed on his bottom lip thoughtfully before nodding. "You're right."

Mr. Cloy hobbled along the edge of the roof and shouted down into the street. He waved his hand over his head and then hobbled back to the far edge of the building to draw the dead from the main street.

"Lenore, Ken, I got them right under me and they are looking like they wanna climb the wall and get me. You two better get going now while the front street is clear." Mr. Cloy looked painfully-pale and fragile as he gave them a small wave.

"Thank you, Leslie," Lenore called out.

"We won't ever forget you. You've been such a great friend!" Ken mimed giving Mr. Cloy a hug.

Mr. Cloy grinned, shaking his head. "I guess the rapture comes a little later on. You guys have a fun ride up. I always wondered what it would be like." He sighed and raised his hands over his head. "Come on! Over here. Come look at the human on the roof. Yay! That's it. Come on over!"

The cries and moans from below grew louder as the zombies trapped in the storage room became even more agitated. Lenore couldn't imagine how Mr. Cloy felt with all those things staring at him so hungrily.

Lenore and Ken reluctantly walked away and headed to the door leading downstairs. Just as they began their descent, they looked toward the man who was saving their lives.

"He's such a great guy," Ken said at last.

Lenore nodded, suddenly afraid she was about to cry.

Together, they hurried down the stairs to Ken's apartment. Lenore was anxious to leave, but bit her lip as Ken threw a few personal possessions into a backpack and searched for his cat. He finally found her asleep under his bed and shoved her into a cat carrier.

"You're kidding," Lenore said.

"I'm not leaving Cher," he said firmly.

"Fine!" Lenore couldn't actually argue with him. She was running off after her grandmother when chances were she was already dead. How could she deny Ken his beloved cat? She gazed into the cat carrier to see Cher staring solemnly at her. After a second, the cat yawned and looked bored. "We're both bat shit crazy."

Ken grabbed a heavy golf club from a bag in the hall closet. "Okay, I'm ready."

Lenore grumbled and almost grabbed one for herself. She decided the coat rack had served them well so far, so she abandoned the thought. Ken unlocked the apartment door and they descended the stairs to the door that opened into the shop.

Ken hesitated at the second door. "What if they got in? What if they're in there waiting?"

Lenore trembled with cold chills as adrenaline pumped through her body. "I'll look."

They shifted places. She carefully unlocked the door and cracked it a few inches. She let out a sigh of relief. The shop was just as they had left it. The Sheriff's dead body was still on the floor and the wardrobe was just as they had left it. Cautiously, she pressed the door completely open and edged around the corner to take a quick peek at the back door. It was also still closed.

"We're okay," she assured Ken. Her heart was beating so hard in her chest she couldn't imagine stepping out into the street. Her heart might explode from fright.

She could hear the distant cries of the dead, but the banging on the door had ceased. Mr. Cloy was doing a great job keeping the dead around the corner of the street, but the undead cannibals were still terrifyingly close.

In silence, they set down their things and moved to the wardrobe. They tried to be as quiet as possible and flinched when the wardrobe groaned and banged as they scooted it away from the door. They froze and waited, but none of the dead were drawn to the sound.

Ken snatched Cher's carrier off the floor and hoisted his golf club into a defensive position. Lenore grabbed the trusty coat rack and took a deep breath. Nervously, she stepped to the window, peeked through the curtain and examined the conditions on the street. It was empty of the dead, but the crashed cars were an obstacle. Mr. Cloy's fancy navy-blue truck was parked across the street just beyond the wreckage.

"Okay, get to the truck and get in. Don't freak out. Keep calm and keep moving until you get to the truck." Lenore held the truck keys firmly in her hand and took several deep breaths, trying to calm her nerves.

"I'm scared," Ken whispered as his cat let out a soft, questioning meow.

"Yeah, me, too. But keep moving. Don't slow down. Just go," she ordered. She took a deep breath and forced herself to open the door.

Lenore froze in terror as the sound of the zombies nearby suddenly seemed much louder. For a second, they both didn't move, then Ken barged past her and ran as fast as he could, his cat carrier banging against his side. Cursing all the noise he was making, Lenore forced her body into motion.

Ken was light on his feet and maneuvered easily and swiftly around the cars. Lenore was much slower and she pumped her arms in an effort to move faster. She was barely clearing the first car when Ken reached the truck and scooted around to the passenger side.

Lifting her arm, she punched the button to unlock the truck. To her horror, she also hit the panic button and the truck erupted into shrill shrieks and loud honking.

"Lenore!"

"Shit!" She paused in the middle of the road and fumbled with the keyless entry remote. Valuable seconds rushed by then she found the button and pressed it again, silencing the alarm.

Moans and the sound of many feet took its place.

Lenore fearfully glanced toward the intersection.

Zombies flooded around the corner.

10.
Into Hell

This was definitely one of those damn fool things people in horror movies did to get themselves killed, Lenore thought. Grunting with frustration, she shook off her temporary paralysis and lumbered toward Mr. Cloy's truck.

"Unlock it!" Ken's voice was almost shrill in his panic.

She hit the UNLOCK button this time and kept hitting it as she ran forward, scooting around the abandoned cars, and trying not to slip on the dark red puddles of blood.

Ken whipped the passenger door open, tossed the cat carrier in, and climbed in all in one seamless motion. He scooted across the cab to the driver's door and motioned to her frantically to hurry.

As if she needed urging...

She heard the footfalls of the approaching zombies gaining on her and she didn't need Ken flapping his hand at her like some sort of crazed traffic cop. Her body felt heavy, her large breasts heaving, her solid legs shoving her body forward. She hated running. She hated it with a passion, but the sound of the snarling, hissing zombies drawing closer was more annoying than her heavy bosom painfully jostling around.

"Lenore!" It was Mr. Cloy's voice.

She swung around, wielding the coat rack like a sword and ended up smacking it into the bloodied and torn face of a female zombie scrambling over the trunk of a car to get to her. Lenore smashed the coat rack down on the thing's head a few times, then used the end to shove the zombie off the car and away from her.

"Just run! Just run!" Mr. Cloy's voice urged.

Her eyes flicked upward. Mr. Cloy's tragic form stood on the edge of the building. He was listing to one side and looked scarily like a zombie already.

"Run, Lenore!" His voice was ragged, but fierce.

The zombies scrambled around the cars, coming straight for her. She whipped around and ran the last few feet to the truck. Ken threw open the driver's door for her and scrambled into his seat. Turning, she threw the coat rack at the zombie three feet from her. Its feet tangled around the coat rack, and it fell. As it thrashed around, trying to get up, other zombies tripped over it, forming a writhing, moaning pile of dead flesh.

Lenore heaved her body into the driver's seat and slammed the door shut just as a horribly disfigured woman threw herself against it. Ken promptly locked the doors, sealing them safely inside.

Lenore sat in silence for a few moments drawing in deep ragged breaths. Beside her, Ken stared at the female zombie clawing at the windshield.

"Can we go now?" His voice was small.

Lenore slid the keys into the ignition, then shook her head. "I don't know how to drive a stick."

"Okay, switch!" Ken scrambled forward and over her.

Cussing under her breath, Lenore slid over to let him behind the wheel. The steady thump of the zombies slapping their hands against the truck made her stomach churn and she avoided looking at the snarling faces outside the passenger door. The truck was either rocking from the zombies' assault or all the trouble she and Ken had moving about so he could get into the driver's seat.

"Ouch, I need those!" Ken slapped at her hand as she tried to shove him off her.

Lenore just snorted and tried not to end up groping him again. Finally, she managed to squeeze into the passenger seat over the damn console wedged between the seats and got her legs adjusted on either side of Cher's carrier. The cat peered up at her through the grate and let out a low hiss.

"Don't make me feed you to the zombies," Lenore threatened.

Ken settled himself into the driver's seat and fumbled with the seat settings.

"Ken!"

"My feet aren't reaching!"

The zombies smashed their hands against the doors and windows over and over again. Blood and chunks of flesh smeared the windows. Some of the zombies were munched down to the bone and one was thumping its stumpy wrist against the windshield over and over again.

"I want to go now, Ken! Now!"

Ken's seat whined as he adjusted it and he screamed at her, "Hold on!"

"Zombies, Ken. Zombies trying to eat us. Let's go!"

The seat finally seemed to be in the right position for Ken's feet to reach the pedals and he turned on the engine. It roared to life, as did the radio. Both Ken and Lenore screamed at the sound of Kenny Roger's voice booming out of the speakers. Lenore reached out and punched the radio off.

"Oh, God, my heart hurts," Ken exclaimed.

Lenore hit him in the arm.

"OUCH! That hurt!"

"Them zombies eating your sweet flesh is gonna hurt a lot more. Drive or I will hit you again!"

Lenore was determined not to die today and that was that.

Ken shifted gears and cautiously drove forward. Lenore gripped the dashboard. The zombies were all around them now, moaning and howling, their disgusting bloodied hands clawing at the car. The cat let out a low yowl of disapproval and Lenore silently agreed with her.

The situation was getting fucked.

Ken carefully maneuvered the truck around the cars blocking the street. He was obviously nervous driving such a big vehicle. They both held their breath as Ken squeezed the truck between two cars. There was a loud screech as the back of the truck caught one of the vehicles. Lenore twisted around in her seat to look out the rear window. Some of the zombies were holding onto the truck bed. Maybe they were trying to stop the truck, or maybe hoping to be carried along with it.

"We're a freaking Happy Meal on wheels," Lenore said with a frown.

Ken grimaced as he inadvertently ran over a few mangled zombies crawling on the ground. "Oh, God, Lenore!"

"They ain't people no more! Don't freak out!"

Ken nodded and edged past a police car, driving close to Mr. Cloy's store.

Pushing on the horn, Ken honked twice and waved to the silhouette of Mr. Cloy on the roof above them. Lenore waved too, but she only caught a glimpse of their friend.

There was a crash as something hit the truck bed and the vehicle rocked violently. Ken screamed and mashed on the brakes. Lenore whipped around to see Mr. Cloy's body fall off the back of the truck. Blood was splattered all over the interior of the truck bed.

"Mr. Cloy!"

"Go," Lenore said.

"Was he dead? Was he a zombie and trying to get to us? Did he kill himself?"

"Just go, Ken!" Lenore yelled at him. "Just go!"

Tears wet her cheeks as she gripped the back of her seat tightly. As Ken drove on, she watched zombies gathering around the fallen form of their friend. She clenched her eyes shut and tried to erase the vision of his battered body from her mind.

Main Street loomed before them. The living dead were scattered along its length. Some moved surprisingly fast in the direction of the truck. These zombies were less damaged than their much-slower counterparts. In some cases, it took more than one look to realize they were dead. The worst of the slow ones was the upper half of an old woman that dragged herself around the corner by her bloodied fingertips.

Ken accelerated away from the shops and drove through the middle of town. His sobs filled her ears as his cat meowed in fear. The truck lurched a few times as they ran over one of the undead and the zombies lashed out at the truck as they passed.

"Why did he jump, Lenore? Why?"

"Maybe he was done with this crazy ass world, Ken. I dunno. He was bit. He was as good as dead. We all knew it."

Ken gripped the steering wheel with one hand as he wiped his face with the other. "I don't know how to get to your house."

"I'll tell you," Lenore said. "And we're going the long way. I don't want any of those things following us."

The truck continued down Main Street and, one by one, the zombies they passed turned to follow.

11.
Hell Sucks

Ken hated this new world. He hated it with a vengeance. It made him sick to his stomach. He just wanted to go home, go back to bed and start the day all over again. Of course, that was not an option. Instead he was driving his dead friend's truck to the outskirts of town. The plan was to loop around to Lenore's neighborhood using back roads. Hopefully, they would be in time to save her grandmother.

A soft meow drew his attention to his precious little Cher sitting in her cat carrier. She didn't look very happy with the situation and he didn't blame her. Their life together had been relatively calm since the no-good-jerkoff had run away with the boy toy. But that was over and what lay ahead was shrouded in mystery.

Ken hated mysteries.

Lenore was silent beside him, her jaw set, her eyes fastened firmly on the road ahead. His heart went out to her. He couldn't even imagine how she was feeling. Though he was worried about his family far away in Houston, he wasn't as close to them as Lenore was to her grandmother.

The town was tearing itself apart all around them. As he drove, he saw flashes of bloodied figures out of the corner of his eye. Suddenly, a figure darted out in front of the truck. They both screamed just before the truck hit the teenage girl and hurtled her off into the ditch.

"She was one of them, right?" Ken felt like his head was going to explode. "Right, Lenore? She was one of them, right?"

"There was blood on her. If she wasn't one yet, she woulda been," Lenore assured him.

"Oh, God," Ken literally felt his heart pounding in his chest. "I didn't mean to-"

"It's okay. I saw blood on her. I did," Lenore swore. "I saw it."

Ken nodded and swallowed hard. His hands shook as he drove and he tried to get a grip on himself. "Okay."

"I wouldn't lie to you," Lenore said in a firm voice.

"Okay," he said one more time. He bobbed his head up and down in affirmation of his words. "I believe you."

"Circle around on Cemetery Road," Lenore directed.

"Ugh! What if they are coming out of the graves?"

"Then they're probably all out and eating someone by now," Lenore answered without a touch of humor in her voice.

Ken flipped on his turn signal and drove the truck onto a very narrow dirt road. The old cemetery was just that: old. No one was buried there anymore due to restriction of space. Most people from the town were now buried around ten miles out of the city limits in a brand new cemetery with flat headstones and boring landscaping. The old cemetery on Cemetery Road was full of tall gravestones, mausoleums, and weeping angels. It was overgrown with weeds nowadays and the city was constantly harassing the holders of the privately owned land to clean it up.

As Ken drove over the road that was rife with deep gouges, they both lapsed into sullen silence. The cemetery, off to Ken's left, was quiet and devoid of anything living or undead. The high wrought-iron fence leaned dangerously in spots, but the graves were undisturbed. Wherever the zombies had come from, it was not the graveyard.

The appallingly-potholed little road curved around behind the cemetery and under a canopy of gnarled, overgrown oak trees. The branches overhead created deep shadows under the canopy and Ken felt unnerved by the sudden gloom. The silent graveyard loomed in his peripheral vision. Even though he had seen the dead come to life, he was more unnerved by being so close to the hallowed ground of the cemetery.

Cher let out a low, cranky meow.

"It's okay, sugar, we're almost there," Lenore said.

"Where is the shotgun?" Ken asked suddenly. "Mr. Cloy said the shotgun was in the truck."

Lenore looked over her shoulder at the empty gun rack. "It's not in the rack. Must be around here somewhere." She began to feel around behind their seats.

Ken gasped as a zombie stumbled into the area where the old road intersected with the residential street that led to Lenore's house. It was a male, terribly mutilated and missing its eyes. It appeared to hear the truck, for it started to screech.

Ken stomped on the brakes and stared at the creature in horror. Lenore yelped as she fell back into her seat clutching the shotgun.

"Ken!"

"What?"

"Run it over!"

The blind zombie wandered in front of them, its hands reaching out, searching for the truck.

Ken could not believe what he was seeing. The eyeless sockets and empty chest cavity was the stuff of horror movies or an X Files episode. This close, the zombie was almost too much for him to handle.

"Ken, run it over!" Lenore shouted again.

Cher yowled anxiously.

Ken shifted into reverse and pulled away from the zombie. Beside him, Lenore clutched the shotgun in both hands. Shifting gears, he took a deep breath.

"Just floor it and hit it," Lenore instructed.

Ken swallowed and shoved his foot down onto the accelerator. The big truck roared forward and just before it hit the zombie, Ken squeezed his eyes shut.

"Ken!"

The impact was brutal. The truck was slammed to one side and the screech of metal grinding against metal filled the cab. Ken was thrown violently, his seatbelt catching him securely and pinching deep into his chest. The airbags exploded and the air filled with fine white powder.

"What the-" Ken muttered, opening his eyes.

It wasn't the zombie that had smashed into the front of the truck, but a small car. Inside, a young woman was draped over the steering wheel. The windshield of her tiny, ancient car was shattered and glass glittered in her blond hair.

Cher hissed loudly as Lenore moaned beside him. Ken straightened in his seat as Lenore raised her hand to her bleeding temple. She appeared dazed.

"We need to get that girl and..." Ken's voice trailed off. The front end of the truck wasn't that badly crumpled, but it was listing to one side. He shifted gears quickly and tried to reverse. The truck didn't budge. The tire was most likely rammed into the side of the wheel well and was not budging.

"What the hell just happened?" Lenore said in a slurred voice.

"An accident and-No! No! No!"

The zombie he had been trying to hit hauled itself over the hood of the small car toward the shattered windshield. Its grotesquely gnawed fingers anxiously sought flesh. Another zombie, this one a woman in a pale pink housecoat, also reached the car embedded into the side of the truck, and tried to reach the unconscious girl.

"Lenore! Lenore! We have to shoot them! Give me the gun!"

She just stared at him blankly, still woozy.

Ken snatched the shotgun out of her hands and fumbled with it. He didn't have the slightest idea how to work the weapon. He feverishly searched for something labeled a *safety*. The characters on TV always talked about it on cop shows. He knew it had to be loaded and ready. Mr. Cloy always said he kept his weapons locked and loaded.

He found a button and pushed it.

The shotgun went off with a thunderous roar. The driver's side window exploded beside him, showering him with glass. Deafened by the shot, Ken couldn't even hear himself screaming.

Outside, the female zombie managed to grab the girl's hair and began pulling her toward her. Ken could feel his heart pounding as he tried to aim the shotgun at the female zombie. Just as he squeezed the trigger, the shotgun was knocked to the side.

The blast caught the unconscious girl in the car full in the chest.

Ken gasped.

A hand, bloodied and chewed, thrust into the truck's broken window, grabbing for him.

12.
It Gets Worse

When Ken fired through the window, Lenore jerked upright and felt her brain careen wildly inside her skull. She gripped her head tightly between her hands and moaned softly. Between being deaf and her head feeling like it was about to explode, she felt alert once more.

She had an inkling she may have been knocked unconscious for a few moments. The disorientation she felt after the crash was fading now. The world seemed to be coming out of the haze. Instead of feeling like she was moving in slow motion through a horror movie, she felt painfully-aware of the world in action around her.

Ken screamed beside her and she turned to see a hand reaching through the shattered window. He thrashed around in his seat trying to evade the zombie.

Lenore leaned over, still feeling rather sluggish, and saw the zombie try to grab Ken. "Help me! Help me!" Ken struggled with the seatbelt.

Lenore pulled the shotgun off his lap.

"I fired two shots! It doesn't have any more!"

She took aim at the horrible shredded face and pulled the trigger. The shotgun thundered and the zombie fell. The other zombies paid no attention as they continued to pull apart the girl in the car.

"It's dead. Calm down." Lenore's fingers found the button on his buckle and pressed it.

Ken nearly crawled onto her lap trying to get away from the shattered driver side window.

Lenore fumbled for the bag she had pulled the shotgun out of. More zombies were struggling to get into the car that had crashed into them. The feeding frenzy had the attention of the undead. For now they weren't paying mind to the truck or its occupants. Lenore snagged the bag and yanked it onto her lap. Checking inside, she was relieved to see several boxes of shotgun shells.

"Lenore, Lenore, I killed that girl they're eating. I killed her," Ken whispered in a trembling voice.

"Can't worry about that now," Lenore answered and shoved the passenger door open. She dropped out of the truck and surveyed the surroundings. She heaved the bag over one shoulder and held the shotgun in one hand.

"Zombies, everywhere, Lenore," Ken hissed.

"Window broken. Broken truck. Get out." Lenore's head was throbbing and her vision was a little off, but she knew they had to go and now.

Ken slid out of the truck and dragged his bag with him. He snagged Cher's carrier. He looked too pale and his eyes were huge in his pinched face.

From behind the battered cars came the terrible sounds of the feeding frenzy. The crunching and slurping was enough to make anyone want throw up, but Lenore's tummy was empty now. She swallowed firmly and pulled Ken along behind her.

She could see her home just three houses down the block to the right. It was so close. If they could just avoid any of the really fast zombies, they could probably make it to safety.

Ken breathed heavily beside her as they jogged toward the house. Though she didn't want to, she reluctantly took a quick peek behind them. A badly-mauled zombie trailed behind them. Its leg was chewed to the bone and it was missing an arm. It was Mr. Thames, her elderly neighbor, who had been tending his yard when she had left for work not too long ago.

Whipping about, she aimed the shotgun at his head and pulled the trigger. The shotgun merely clicked. It was empty.

"Crap!"

"Reload it!"

"Do you know how?"

"No," Ken whispered.

Lenore flipped the shotgun around and held it by its warm barrel as Mr. Thames drew closer.

"Let's run!"

"It will follow us!"

Ken sobbed while he clutched the cat carrier even tighter in his arms.

"I'm gonna hit its head," Lenore said. She blinked her eyes, trying to focus on the task. "I'll hit him until he doesn't move, then we run to the house."

She saw Ken nod wildly beside her. Lenore fought back fear and concentrated her attention on the zombie. Beyond the walking remains of Mr. Thames, she could see more zombies gathering around the accident, feasting on what was left of that poor girl in the car. It was only a matter of time before they saw Ken and Lenore.

Ken unexpectedly let out a frantic, awful noise and rushed Mr. Thames. He shoved Cher's cat carrier into the old man's chest, toppling him over. The zombie tried to grab onto Ken, but her friend skirted away, clutching the carrier tight as Cher caterwauled angrily.

"Hit him, Lenore! Hurry!"

Lenore danced around Mr. Thames's grasping hands and smashed the butt of the shotgun down onto his head. It made a horrible noise as his skull shattered and dented in. Yet, he continued to grab at her. Lenore slammed it down a second time and busted in the front of Mr. Thames's face. It was shocking to see his features vanish beneath her blow in a gout of blood. She hit him one more time and finally he stopped thrashing.

"Run! Run! Run!" Ken screamed. He turned and ran.

A swift look down the street told the horrible story. The zombies had seen them and were coming. Some struggled just to walk, while others easily leapt up and started to sprint toward Lenore.

Lenore dashed after Ken. Her head swam a bit as she struggled to keep running in a straight line toward her grandmother's house. Cussing under her breath, she clutched the empty shotgun tightly in her hands. She would not die today without a fight.

"The blue house, Ken!" she shouted. "Run to the blue house!"

Ken darted across the lawn to the house and started banging on the front door.

Lenore forced breath into her painfully-constricting lungs, but it was getting harder to run. Her body felt so heavy and her head felt like it was about to fall off her shoulders.

"Please, please, please," she prayed.

She was almost to the front yard of the house when she heard the first gunshot. She let out a wheezing gasp and spun around to see that the zombies were still in pursuit. A few broke off the main pack toward Tito Hernandez, Olympia's son. Her grandmother's best friend was nowhere to be seen, but her son was on the lawn of her home firing at the zombies. He was snarling out cusswords in Spanish as he deftly fired at the running crowd. His short form was rippling with muscles and sweat beaded on his tan skin. His short black hair glistened wetly from the oil he always used to slick it back and his sunglasses hid his dark eyes.

"Run, Lenore, run!" He continued to fire and reload calmly.

The zombies fell beneath his bullets, but there were at least five still heading straight for him.

Ken continued to bang on the door. "Let us in! Let us in!"

Lenore reached the walk up to the house and huffed and puffed her way up to the steps. Checking over her shoulder, she saw the zombies struggling to maneuver over the white picket fence bordering the Hernandez house. The zombies had forgotten about Lenore and were focused on the Hispanic man. Tito continued to pick them off one by one. He was coolly efficient and brutal with his accuracy.

"Do you have your key?" Ken was gasping loudly.

"Yeah, hold on," she answered, and handed him the bloodied shotgun. She fumbled around in her jean pockets while Cher, the very upset kitty, meowed loudly.

"Where is my Mama?" Tito's voice was surprisingly close. He was already running up the walk. Behind him the street was littered with dead zombies.

Lenore managed to grab the key out of her pocket and shoved into the lock. "I don't know."

"Is she with your grandma?" Tito reloaded his pistol and looked around uneasily.

"I don't know," Lenore said and unlocked the front door.

"Be careful, Lenore," Tito said to her. "Open it slowly."

Lenore swallowed and nodded. She gently pressed the door open. Her grandmother came into view. She was lying on the floor; face down, the phone still clutched in one hand. Without thinking, Lenore rushed to her side and fell to her knees. "Grandma!"

Ken stumbled in, clutching the cat carrier, and looking around. "Lenore, be careful! She might be a zombie!"

Tito stepped just inside the front door. "Lenore, be careful, *chica*. Seriously. This shit is whacked out. Back up."

"What he said," Ken agreed.

Lenore blinked back tears and shook her head. "No, not my grandma. No." Her voice sounded wrong to her. It was muffled by emotion and the damn ringing in her ears.

Tito appeared about to say something when Lenore saw a figure lurch into view behind him.

"Tito!" Lenore's voice sounded shrill to her own ears.

The tiny Mexican man whirled about as his mother stepped onto the porch behind him.

"Mama?"

The old woman opened her mouth and blood spilled over her lips as she let out a hungry moan. Grabbing onto Tito, the old woman moved in swiftly for a bite.

13.
Trapped

"On my gawd!" Ken shrieked as he stumbled away from the door.

Tito didn't say a word as he lifted his pistol and fired a shot straight up through the old woman's neck as she lunged forward to bite him. A fountain of blood and brain matter erupted from the rear of her head. The silent zombie slid to the porch in a heap.

Rotating sharply, Tito shoved Ken further into the house. Without a word, he locked the screen door, shut the heavy wood door, and bolted it shut.

Ken stood in the foyer, clutching the yowling cat's carrier to his chest. Lenore stared in shock at Tito. The Hispanic man walked rapidly across the living room, fell into a recliner, raised the hand still clutching the pistol to his forehead, and began to pray in Spanish.

Lenore couldn't imagine what he was feeling. She had felt as if the world had ended the second she saw her grandmother lying on the floor of their tiny little house. Her heart had literally skipped a beat in her chest. Looking at her grandmother's fallen form, she knew she had to find out if she was alive or dead. She picked up a heavy leaded glass bowl from the coffee table, dumped out the plastic fruit, and moved to her grandmother's side.

Kneeling next to the woman who had raised her with a firm hand and a loving smile, Lenore could barely breathe. Her ribs suddenly felt too tight for her body and her chest hurt. Her grandmother's face looked peaceful as if she was sleeping.

"I don't see any blood," Lenore whispered to Ken. Her hand clutched the heavy glass bowl at her side, ready to strike. But would she be able to?

Ken remained motionless, breathing heavily, his eyes wide.

Tito's prayer ended abruptly. Lenore heard the creak of the chair as he stood and his footfalls approaching. The tips of his battered boots came into view as he stood over her grandmother. Lenore raised her head to see he was aiming his pistol over her grandmother's head.

"Put the bowl down. I'll do it if we have to," he said.

Lenore did as he said, then gripped her grandmother's arm. Shaking the old woman, Lenore could feel her own heart pounding even harder. If her grandmother opened her eyes to reveal those terrible milky dead eyes, she didn't think she could hold onto her sanity.

A low, uneven moan issued forth from the old woman's lips.

"Oh, God," Ken whispered.

Tito didn't fire, but Lenore saw his body tense.

"Grandma?" Lenora's voice rasped over the word. "Grandma, wake up!"

Her grandmother sat up swiftly.

Tito and Lenore both jumped back.

"Lord Jesus, save me," her grandmother exclaimed and stared up at them in shock.

Tito let out a long breath and lowered the pistol.

"Grandma, you're alive!" Lenore hugged her tight, relief flooding her.

"Oh, thank God!" Ken threw his arms around both of them.

"I won't be if you keep on squeezing me like this!"

Lenore released her grandmother, her smile so wide she felt as if her cheeks would crack.

Her grandmother straightened her dress and looked around warily. Still woozy, she raised a hand to her head. "Okay, I remember going to the door and seeing..." She fell silent and glanced up at Tito sadly. "There were all sorts of bad stuff on the TV. I didn't think it was here yet. But I saw-"

"I already took care of her," Tito said in a pained tone.

Lenore helped her grandmother stand. She could almost hear the older woman's bones creaking.

"I was on the phone with her and she said someone was at the door. We were in the middle of our soap opera and I wasn't too pleased about her taking off just when Stefano was revealing his evil plans. Then I heard her screaming." Grandma leaned heavily against the back of her sofa and sighed. "I couldn't do nothing, but listen. It was awful."

Tito didn't move, but Lenore saw a tear on his cheek under his dark sunglasses.

"I went to the door and looked out and saw her out there..." Grandma sighed and shook her head. "...on the porch and Mr. Thames was...he was...I guess it was too much. I remember I was gonna go get the gun and then...I think I fainted."

"So none of those things got you in any way or into the house?" Tito asked.

"No. No. I'm sorry, Tito, about your mother."

"Me, too, Grandma." Tito lightly kissed her cheek. "I'm going to double-check the doors and windows. You three stay here."

Lenore lovingly embraced her grandmother, relishing the soft warmth of her body. She was given a firm, tight hug, then released. Ken flung his arms around the old woman and was rewarded with a hug and a kiss on the cheek.

"It's good to see you two are okay. Sorry to scare you, but my blood pressure makes it rough on me sometimes. I better take my pills."

Tito slipped back into the living room. The house was so small it didn't take much time to check it. "Windows and doors are all locked. I closed all the curtains so that they can't see us in here. Better close those, too."

Ken hurried over and slid the heavy velvet curtains over the bay window. They were plunged into an eerie darkness.

"I need my revolver," Grandma decided. "It's under my bed."

"I'll get it," Tito said. "I want you three to stay in this room until I can figure out what to do next."

"You know, we can't stay here," Ken said in a quavering voice. "Once they figure out we are in here, they're gonna get in."

"I know, man. That is why I gotta think," Tito's voice was sharp. "Just let me think, okay?" He walked out of the living room and into the kitchen.

Ken made a face as Tito disappeared and Lenore shook her finger at him. "He just had to kill his own mama."

"He doesn't need to snap my head off. I'm just trying to help!" Ken sulkily sat in a chair, Cher's carrier on his lap, and his bag at his side.

"It's okay, baby. We'll get out of here," Grandma assured him.

Ken's skin was too pale and Lenore was worried about how much he was sweating. She felt completely exhausted, too, but Ken appeared sickly. He was not emotionally resilient. The day was definitely too much for her to bear so she imagined he must be on the verge of a breakdown.

Tito reappeared with the revolver, sliding bullets into the cylinder as he walked. Lenore had forgotten all about the revolver. It had belonged to her grandfather.

"Can you shoot this?"

"I can shoot it," Grandma said confidently. "I can kill those zombies. Trust me. After what I saw them do to Olympia, I can shoot 'em."

Tito nodded as he handed it over.

"I don't know how to reload this," Lenore confessed, pointing to the shotgun. "I beat the zombie with it instead."

Tito's lips quirked into a small smile. "Okay. Let me show you how to do that. Where is the ammo?"

Lenore lifted Mr. Cloy's bag and the shells inside rattled around. For the next few minutes, Tito patiently explained to both her and Ken how to load the shotgun and what they had to do to fire it. Ken seemed to be barely paying attention and looked sleepy. Despite her head hurting so badly she wanted to remove her brain to release the pressure, Lenore felt keenly awake. She shook Ken a few times and he looked at her blearily.

"Keep alert," Lenore ordered him.

Ken nodded. "I need water."

"I'll get it," Grandma said.

"Be careful," Tito ordered.

"I got my revolver. I'm okay," she answered, heading to the kitchen. Her fuzzy pink slippers slapped against the wood floor as she walked.

"What are we going to do now?" Lenore asked Tito.

"Get out of here. Out of the house. Out of town."

"We can take the old caddy in the garage," Lenore decided.

"I was thinking about Mr. Thames's old RV," Tito answered. "He's got that thing in mint condition."

"We'd have to go across the road for that." Fear filled Ken's voice and his eyes seemed even more sunken than before.

"We can do it if we're smart," Tito promised him. "Load up on supplies here, get them into the caddy, drive not to the front of his house, but down the alley in the back to where the RV is, load up, get out of town."

"Sounds good to me," Grandma piped up as she came into the living room holding a tall glass of ice water for Ken. "The zombies are trying to get in the back gate. I think the faster we're out of here, the better."

Ken seized the glass of water and gulped it down like it was vodka. Lenore didn't blame him. Her stomach was quivering with anxiety.

"Let's get packing and moving," Tito said.

Instead of rushing to obey his words, they all stood in silence and listened as some*thing* began to beat on the front door. Fear filled the room. Lenore felt like she was going to choke on it.

"Children, we can't stay here and wait for them to get in. Get moving. Now!" Grandma glowered at them, waving her hands.

Her voice jarred them out of their frozen state and they began to quickly gather anything they would need on the road. Lenore watched Ken hurry to the kitchen, clutching his bag and cat carrier. He still looked bad, but at least he was moving. That gave her hope.

Then a second set of fists began to pound on the screen door and she could hear the metal frame rattling.

Time was running out.

14.
Planning to Escape

Ken stood hopelessly in the kitchen not sure what he should be doing. He couldn't remember what Tito had said. In fact, he was having trouble stringing his thoughts together into anything coherent.

The banging on the front door resounded through the house. Ken couldn't stop shaking uncontrollably and he just wanted to be with Lenore. Standing alone in the kitchen, he felt vulnerable. He sought out Lenore's bedroom, desperate to be safely near her.

He switched Cher's carrier to his other hand and flexed his numb one. He had not realized how hard he had been clutching the handle. Inside the carrier, Cher let out another low hiss of frustration.

"Shh, Cher. It's okay," he lied. He swallowed hard, trying to get the nasty lump out of his throat.

At last he found the bedroom. Inside, Lenore was tossing some of her possessions into a bag. Her expression was a grim reminder of when he had done the exact same thing in his apartment. It wasn't easy packing up a little piece of your life with no idea when – or if - you would return. Lenore had already gone through this once before with Hurricane Rita. She had left for the shelter believing she would have a home to return to, but that had not been the case.

Ken suspected that neither of them would be returning home this time. Zombies trumped hurricanes in the life-ruining category.

"Stop staring at me," Lenore ordered grumpily.

"I can't help it! I'm afraid if I look away I'll lose you."

"You're being a silly girl," Lenore chided. She snatched a magazine photo of Common off her mirror and shoved it into the bag.

Ken sniffled loudly as he realized any chances of either of them finding the man of their dreams were greatly diminished. The world had gone to hell and he was single. Freaking zombies had to ruin everything.

"We're getting out of here and going somewhere safe. So stop crying and be tough." Lenore fixed her stern gaze on him.

Even with a fresh wave of fear washing over him, Ken nodded and squared his shoulders.

Lenore lugged her bag out of the room and into the kitchen. Ken trailed closely behind her.

Tito was in the kitchen throwing canned and boxed food into plastic bags, mumbling in Spanish. He was swift in his movements and he seemed a little more agitated than he had been earlier.

"What's wrong?" Ken shifted uneasily on his feet.

"I got through to my wife. She's visiting family down in Laredo. It's bad there, too. She took off in the car with my kids and my youngest brother. They're having trouble getting out of the area." His words were uttered in a tight, frustrated tone.

Ken felt his stomach tighten. He had the desire to run to the bathroom and throw up. If Tito left them now...

"Go get your grandma. We need to go. More of those things are out there."

Lenore dropped her bag and hurried out of the kitchen to find her grandmother.

"Do you think we can make it?" Ken hated the way his voice cracked.

"No," Tito answered honestly. "But we have to try. I have to get to my family. Chances are it's not gonna happen, but I gotta try. I'm going to get you guys going to a safe place, then take off to find them."

"I don't want to..." Ken hesitated, feeling his bowels complaining at his dark thoughts. Dread was running through his blood. "I don't want to get eaten."

"I'll put down anyone that gets caught by those things," Tito vowed.

Ken felt his intestines twist around. "Uh, is that supposed to be comforting?"

"Do you want to be eaten alive or have a quick exit?" Tito looked at Ken directly in the eyes.

He gulped hard and looked down at Cher in her carrier. "Save my cat if they get me or do her, too." He felt tears, hot and heavy, threatening to spill over his lashes.

Tito nodded curtly. He peeked through a sliver in the curtains. "We got lucky. They've moved on to the Thompson house. The back door is open."

"But that means that the Thompsons are-"

Tito lifted one shoulder. "Yeah. Get used to it, kid. The world is royally fucked now and we gotta keep going." He studied Lenore's big bag on the floor. Without a word, he dumped all her possessions out and shoved the bags of food inside.

Ken started to protest, but thought better of it. Instead, he tried to put as much of her stuff into his already bulging bag.

From within her carrier, Cher hissed her disapproval at the whole process.

Lenore escorted her grandma into the kitchen. Ken saw her eyes flash with anger at Tito's actions, but she held her tongue. Silently, she reached down and plucked the picture of Common up off the floor. She stuffed it in her jean pocket.

"I need my medicine," Grandma whispered. There was an ashy undertone to her dark skin and her eyes looked a little glazed. She leaned against a counter and looked more fragile than she had a few minutes earlier.

Lenore immediately opened a drawer and pulled out several bottles. Tito filled up a glass with water for the older woman. The room was thick with tension as they all watched Lenore's grandmother swallow her pills. The thumping on the front door was starting to fray Ken's last nerve.

"I'll be okay," the older woman reassured them. "I just got a little upset. I could hear...Emily Thompson screaming." She raised her hand and pressed it to her chest. "It just..."

"We're going to get in the car and we're going to go," Tito said firmly. "I want all of you to stay calm."

Ken's heart was beating inside of his ribcage so hard it hurt. He just wanted to sit down and cry.

"I'm ready," Lenore said in a determined voice. "I'm ready to go."

"Maybe we could stay here and-" Lenore's grandmother started to say in a tremulous voice.

Somewhere in the house, glass shattered and something large made a terrible racket as it fell. A low, terrifying moan reverberated through the house.

"The air conditioner in grandma's bedroom," Lenore stated simply. "It fell out of the window."

"Time to go," Tito said and headed in the direction of the door to the outside.

The garage was an add-on to the small house and accessible by a door that opened to a short sidewalk. Someone had erected a trellis on either side of the walkway for the sake of privacy. Ivy crawled up the latticework to create a green screen. The recent winter months had taken its toll on the ivy and it was just now beginning to flourish again.

Tito hesitated as he looked out the window at the short walkway to the garage. "The garage door is shut, right?"

"Yeah," Lenore assured him.

"And it's got an electric door opener?"

"Uh, no."

Tito's shoulders tensed slightly, then he nodded. "Okay, here is the plan. I'm going first. When I open the door into the garage, Grandma then Ken goes through. Lenore, you come last. You carry the shotgun. When we get into the garage, Grandma and Ken, get into the backseat of the car-"

"I get carsick in the back," Ken protested before he realized how ridiculous that sounded.

Tito gave him a fierce look, then continued. "Lenore, open the passenger door. I'll open the driver's door. You stand right next to the passenger door and cover me while I open the garage door. As soon as it's up far enough for the car to get through, we both get into the car, and get out of here. Everyone got that?"

Ken nodded even though he felt a little confused. His body wouldn't stop shaking and it was beginning to annoy him. He hoisted his bag onto his shoulder and switched the cat carrier to his other hand. His stomach was knotting again. If only he could have a few minutes to sit down and catch his breath.

"This is gonna be simple. Okay? We do this and we get out of here," Tito said in a calm voice. He snatched the keys hanging next to the back of the door. "Now, which key is what?"

Lenore stepped forward and showed him. Tito yanked all the rest of the keys off and left the only two that mattered hanging on the ring. Lenore's grandmother was still leaning against the counter, but she looked a little better than she had moments ago.

Tito grabbed the bag of food and slung it over his strong shoulders. He was a small man, but he was finely muscled from either hard work or good workouts. Tito regarded the three people staring at him with a slight smile on his lips.

"C'mon. Today is fucked up enough. It can't get much worse." He unlocked the door and opened it.

Sunlight streamed in through the trellis on either side of the walkway. It was an almost-serene scene. The garage door, painted a light blue, waited on the other side.

"See. Easy." Tito stepped out onto the sidewalk.

Instantly, hands reached through the trellis.

15.
Escape

His gun arm captured by the zombie, Tito swore angrily. Lenore and Ken froze in terror as a creature with no face struggled to pull Tito's arm through the trellis. Grandma raised her revolver and fired a single shot. Lenore jumped, startled by the sound.

"Grandma!"

"Got 'em," Grandma said triumphantly.

The shot had splintered the trellis near the zombie's head and the corpse hung limply against it. Ken mouthed the word "wow" as he gazed at Grandma in surprise.

Tito swore as he pried the now truly dead thing's fingers from his arm. "C'mon! Get into the garage!"

Lenore ducked into the ivy-draped walkway, ignoring the dead zombie listing against it. Out of the corner of her eye she saw more zombies stumbling toward them. She pushed Ken along with one hand, clutching the shotgun with the other.

"Move it!"

"Be careful of Grandma!" Ken snapped back.

Tito deftly unlocked the door and ducked into the garage. Her grandmother glowered at the zombies moving toward the walkway for a moment before following him inside.

"Never liked monsters. Always mucking things up," Grandma muttered from the humid darkness inside the garage.

Reaching the doorway, Ken shifted the cat carrier as he tried to get his huge bag through the narrow opening.

Lenore heard the zombie before she saw it. The hard slap of its feet against the asphalt accompanied by its grunts drew her attention through the lattice toward the front of the house. The zombie raced up the driveway then veered off to head directly toward her.

"I ain't dying today!"

Lenore shoved Ken through the door, sending him sprawling as Cher yowled in her carrier. She barely managed to get through the doorway before the zombie burst through the flimsy wood and vines, sending splinters and leaves flying. Whipping around, Lenore caught the door with one hand as the disoriented zombie twisted about looking for her. Just as it spotted her, snarling, blood foaming around its torn lips, Lenore slammed the door in its face.

"Lock it!" Tito ordered.

Fumbling with the lock, Lenore jumped as the zombie hit the other side. Tito slammed into the door next to her, bracing it with one shoulder as she managed to twirl the doorknob lock and the deadbolt.

"Ken, get in the car now!" Tito let go of the trembling door long enough to seize an old wheelbarrow and shove it up against it.

The door was old, thick wood, but the hinges and locks were rusted and flimsy. It wouldn't last long under the constant assault of the undead.

"This could complicate things," Tito muttered.

"Ya think?" Lenore raised an eyebrow.

"We'll move fast," Tito answered, daring to release his hold on the door. "Cover me."

Lenore stepped away the vibrating door, her eyes flicking toward the hinges. She could see the screws slowly working loose.

"Make it super-fast," Lenore said to Tito.

Inside the car, Ken and Grandma pulled on their seatbelts as Cher wailed. Lenore yanked the passenger door open as Tito matched her actions on the driver's side. Leaning in, he fit the key into the ignition and started the car. After a cough and a stutter, the old car's engine rumbled to life.

"I'm going to open it now." Tito took a deep breath while heading over to the garage door. "Cover me."

Lenore swallowed as the sound of the zombies pounding on the side door filled the small garage. The noise grew even louder as more fists began to bang against the garage walls.

"They know we're in here now," Tito moaned. "Dammit! Lenore, shoot anything that moves. Just make sure it's not me!" Cracking his knuckles, Tito leaned down and gripped the lever for the garage door. "Couldn't have an electric door, huh?"

"Grandma is too cheap," Lenore grumbled.

"Once it gets going, it'll slide right up!" Grandma called out.

Lenore checked the safety on the shotgun. It felt awkward in her grip and she felt useless with it. She had no real idea what the hell she was doing, but she knew for sure that she was not going to get eaten by those things.

Behind her, she heard the whine of one of the car windows descending. Looking over her shoulder, she saw her grandmother, seated behind the driver's seat, leaning out the window clutching her revolver.

"Open that door! Let's get out of here before those things get in!" Grandma shouted.

With a grunt, Tito yanked up on the door, the old rollers creaking and groaning as they slid upward along the old tracks. Bright sunlight billowed under the door, harsh and blinding. It took Lenore's eyes a second to adjust as the door rolled back. Tito had already fired into the face of a zombie by the time her vision cleared. Another was crawling toward him on the nubs of its wrists. Lenore aimed and fired.

A tuft of grass from the front yard sailed into the air and landed near the crawling zombie.

"Hit the zombie, Lenore!" Tito shouted, shoving another zombie off its feet.

A small crowd of zombies were coming up the drive and Tito backed away quickly.

"I can't shoot 'em with you in the way!" Grandma yelled, waving at him to move.

Muttering in Spanish, Tito darted around the open car door. A zombie followed, smashing into it as it tried to grab Tito. The door started to close, pinning Tito to the side of the car. His gun spun away, disappearing behind some boxes piled near the door. Using one hand, Tito gripped the zombie's throat, holding off the snapping teeth.

Lenore swung the shotgun around and took aim.

"No, don't!" Tito cried out, terrified.

She fired.

The zombie's head jerked to one side as it fell out of sight.

Tito looked at her with surprise, but quickly climbed into the car, banging the door shut. Sliding into the front seat, Lenore grabbed hold of the passenger door.

"Close it! Close it! Close it!" Ken screamed in his most girly voice. Cher yowled in agreement.

Lenore tried to pull the door shut, but it caught. Looking down, she saw the handless zombie had wedged its head up under the door and was trying to climb into the car. Panicking, Lenore scrabbled at the shotgun.

She was deafened by the gun going off near her head. Later, she would swear she felt the heat of the blast and saw the bullet go arcing past her to smash into the head of the zombie.

"Shut the door!" Grandma shouted, her revolver in her hand.

"Damn, Grandma! You're fierce!" Tito exclaimed.

Ken whimpered.

Lenore reached out to grab the door again just as the side door into the garage slammed open. Zombies poured in, moving swiftly toward her. Her sweaty fingers fumbled with the latch as she tried to shut the door. She could see far too clearly the first zombie barreling toward her, its broken and hungry mouth opened wide to bite as its hands lashed out to grip her.

The car lurched forward, plowing through the zombies in the driveway. The passenger door slammed shut with the momentum. The old car barreled down the short drive, tossing zombies off the hood. Tito spun the steering wheel sharply to the left, the back of the car fishtailing for a second before the tires gripped the road and they surged forward.

The neighborhood was in chaos. People fled on foot from the wreck of a car that had crashed into a van. Swift-footed zombies were in pursuit as the slower undead clawed at the doors and windows of the smashed vehicles.

"We gotta help them!" Lenore cried out.

"Can't! We gotta keep moving or die," Tito answered tersely.

"Those poor people go to my church!" Grandma protested.

"We stop, we die."

"I don't want to die," Ken said emphatically. "Really don't want to die!"

Lenore twisted around in her seat to see that the small group of people was quickly being cornered by the zombies in the neighborhood. She saw what Tito said was true, but the twisting pain in her gut and throat told her it wasn't right. Closing her eyes, she looked forward, unable to watch.

Tito avoided a pack of zombies and the car whipped around the corner. Lenore took a deep breath and watched the road, her eyes rimmed with tears.

Taking a hard left, Tito directed the old boat of a car into the alley, speeding along toward the RV parked behind Mr. Thames' house.

"Do you know where the keys to the RV are?" Ken asked from the backseat.

Tito shrugged.

"That isn't what I want to hear," Lenore snapped.

"Cause if those keys are on Mr. Thames, I think he is busy eating those people from my church right now." Grandma's voice was harsh.

"Actually, I killed him earlier," Lenore mumbled.

"Oh," Grandma said. "Oh."

"It doesn't matter if there are keys or not. I can get in." Tito gave a little shrug. "I was a bad kid for a few years in my teens. I got...skills."

The car rolled to a stop beside the RV. Tito quickly leaped out. "Stay here. I'm going to scout it out. Lenore, get behind the wheel just in case." Before anyone could protest, he darted around the RV and disappeared.

Lenore slid into the driver's seat, grumbling the whole way. Gripping the steering wheel, she stared down the surprisingly-quiet alley.

"What if he doesn't come back?" Ken asked from the backseat.

Lenore slowly exhaled. "We better pray he does. The car is almost out of gas."

16.
Fear

Ken could barely catch his breath. His chest felt so tight he could barely stand it. With Cher's carrier wedged between him and the seat in front of him, he supposed that could be part of his problem. But he was pretty sure it was the sound of the zombies nearby that was about to give him a full-fledged heart attack. He wasn't sure if it was better to die with his heart exploding or not. Of course, getting eaten by zombies wasn't a pleasant thought either.

"Take deep breaths, son," Grandma instructed him.

"It hurts," he complained.

"Do it anyway," she said, patting his hand. "Take a deep breath and let it out slow."

Ken obeyed because Lenore was giving him a sharp look over her shoulder. He drew in a deep, shuddering breath, then slowly exhaled. To his surprise, the tightness in his chest lessened and his heart slowed a bit. He took another long drag of the warm air in the car and immediately started choking on a strand of Cher's fur. Coughing violently, he heard Cher hiss as Grandma whacked his back.

"Only you could screw up breathing," Lenore muttered from the front seat.

"I'm sorry!" Ken coughed out, still gagging on the fur stuck in his throat.

He was pretty sure he was turning bright red when Tito ran around the RV. He was holding a crowbar in one hand. Something red and chunky was dripping from one end. Tito yanked the driver's door open and leaned in.

"I can't find the keys and the zombies are coming in the front door of the house. I got the back door barricaded, but we got only a few minutes before they're out here. I'm gonna jimmy the door and hotwire the RV. The second you hear the RV turn on, I want out you out of the car and into the RV. Don't get out of the car until you hear the engine. If things get bad, you may need to take off. I'll follow you in the RV."

"We're almost out of gas," Lenore informed Tito.

"Shit!" He ran his hand over his slick hair. "Just stick to the plan." He shoved the door shut and loped around the back of the RV to work on the door on the other side.

Ken felt his chest tighten again and his breath caught in his fur coated throat. Silence filled the car as Lenore dragged the shotgun onto her lap. Beside him, Grandma checked her revolver one more time. All Ken had as any sort of weapon was Cher's carrier. He stared at his feisty, angry feline and felt like sobbing. He didn't want her to die. He didn't want to die either.

"I really hate today," he wailed before he could catch himself.

"You and me both," Lenore agreed.

"I can't say I'm fond of it either, honey." Grandma shook her head sorrowfully.

The old RV's engine suddenly chugged to life beside the car. A poof of dark smoke burst out of the back of it as Tito revved up the gas.

"Let's go!" Lenore ordered.

She swung her body out of the driver's side as Grandma popped open the back door. Ken fumbled with the lock and latch on his door, his chest hurting with anxiety. Looking up, he saw a zombie on the other side of the chain link fence bordering the alley. The creature was shaking the metal mesh violently, its mouth open in a long wail. The door swung open and Ken almost fell out as he tried to maneuver himself, Cher's carrier and his bag out of the car. Lenore grabbed the bag of food as Grandma hurried around the back of the RV.

"Oh, Jesus, they're coming!" the old woman cried out.

The revolver fired twice as Ken got his legs under him and finally yanked his bag out of the back seat. Sweat pouring down his face, his breath ragged in his ears, he ran around the car, ignoring the growling zombie just a few feet away on the other side of the fence. Lenore was ahead of him, running with the big bag over her shoulder.

As he came around the back end of the RV, he saw the zombies Tito had warned them about struggling through the unhinged back door and shattered windows of Mr. Thames's house. The undead creatures fought with each other to get through the openings and to the humans trying to escape. Ken felt his breath catch in his throat as one of the zombies broke free from the tangle of legs and arms and ran straight for him.

A bullet slammed into the zombie, knocking its head back with the impact. Its body flopped like a rag doll as it fell to the ground and tumbled to a stop.

"Hurry up, boy!" Grandma yelled from the doorway of the RV.

Lenore grabbed his arm and jolted him out of his frozen state. Together they rushed to the open door. Tito appeared in the doorway holding Grandma's gun and fired a few more shots at the pursuing zombies. Lenore tossed the bag in then clambered up into the RV. Ken knew he was hyperventilating, but couldn't stop it. He could barely see straight as he threw his bag inside and lifted Cher's carrier up into his arms as he tried to get in. Tito's strong hand gripped his shoulder and dragged him inside, firing into the face of a zombie about to take a bite out of Ken's back.

"Get him away from the door!" Tito ordered, taking another shot.

Grandma grabbed Cher's carrier as Lenore grabbed Ken's shirt, yanking him away from Tito. The heat inside the vehicle was overwhelming and Ken felt like he was going to faint. He felt something grab his foot and screamed. A child zombie had reached in to grab his pant leg and was trying to climb. Tito kicked the kid's head, knocking him back out.

"Lenore, you gotta drive! I need to watch the door! I broke the latch getting in!"

"Crap!"

"You can do it, honey," her grandmother assured her.

Ken lay on the floor, Cher staring at him through the door of her cat carrier with an accusatory look. Struggling to breathe, he crawled to a nearby chair. He pitched into it as the RV took off with a mighty jolt. Tito braced himself in the doorway of the RV and fired the last shots of the revolver. He tossed it onto the counter nearby and grabbed up the crowbar. Some of the faster zombies paced the RV as Lenore drove down the alley.

"Faster, *chica!*" Tito ordered. He shoved another zombie off its feet as it tried to make a dive for the door.

Lenore's grumbling was loud and angry from the driver's seat, but the RV picked up speed. "Hold on!"

The vehicle swung out of the alley far too fast and Ken screamed as he held on for dear life. Tito looked dangerously close to falling out of the RV for just a second. Another zombie took a swipe at him and Tito kicked it in the face.

"Where do I go?" Lenore shouted over the sound of the wind whistling through the open doorway.

"Not near downtown!" Ken wheezed at her.

"Take this street straight out to the old farm road. Don't slow down, Lenore. They're thick out there," Tito instructed

Tito stared out into the chaos of the world, his powerful muscles tight under his shirt as he gripped the doorway with both hands. The crowbar glistened with blood. Ken couldn't help but stare at the man with awe. He hated that he was falling apart. In his imagination, he had always believed himself to be stronger than this. Slowly, his gaze was drawn to the world beyond Tito.

The small town was in shambles. Houses were on fire. Cars were snarled pieces of metal crashed into sign posts or each other. Screams of terror filled the air mingling with the groans of the dead. Boarded up houses were under attack by the undead as other living people tried to escape on foot or in cars. In the distance, he saw a man on a bicycle pedaling as fast as he could just ahead of a crowd of pursuing zombies.

"Where are we going?" he finally asked. "We can't go to another town."

"Into the hills," Tito finally said. "Up into the hills far away from the towns."

"What about your family?" Ken swallowed hard, unable to imagine what Tito was going through.

"I don't know," Tito said after a long pause. "I don't know."

17.
The Dead Are Coming

Lenore's hands were cramping. Her grip on the steering wheel kept slipping and she cursed her sweaty palms. Tightening her hold, she stared out the dirty windshield at the world that was slowly falling apart. The old RV was almost out of town, but they weren't in the clear yet.

Hordes of the undead were wandering the streets. The walking dead were attacking anyone foolish enough to be on foot. The gruesome zombies also charged cars and tried to break into buildings. Gunshots cracked through the morning air as smoke drifted over the road, briefly obscuring her view. It was like driving through a horror movie.

Two zombies flailed at the RV as she passed, slapping their hands against her window. She gave a little start and muttered a curse, but she kept her eyes on the road and her hands steady. Freaking out while driving would not be a good thing. It would get them killed.

Lenore wished she was still sleeping and that she would wake up in her cozy bed. Her mind snagged the idea and tried to cling to it. Shaking her head, she forced the enticing daydream out of her thoughts. It was crazy to hope for something that could never happen. She had to remain focused on what was happening right now. Frowning, she concentrated on the road.

"You doing a good job, Lenore," her grandmother encouraged her from her perch on the passenger seat.

"I'm scared to death," Lenore admitted as she swerved around a car that had crashed into a truck.

A zombie lurched from the wreck. It was a man and he was chewing on what looked like someone's arm. Bits of flesh and smears of blood stained his shirt. He let out a howl, stretching his hand out toward the RV as they sped by.

Another block and they would be past the last few businesses and houses on the road and heading out of town.

"Look at that," Grandma said, her voice awed yet horrified.

Lenore glanced to the side long enough to see a small crowd of zombies rocking a trailer. She briefly saw a man and woman shooting at the zombies from the windows. More of the undead were staggering or running toward the trailer, drawn by the sound of gunfire.

"Just keep going, Lenore. Don't do any sightseeing. It ain't worth it," Tito called out from behind her. "Just the same shit over and over again."

"Yeah, zombies. Lots of them...eating...people..." Ken added in a broken voice.

The RV had almost cleared the last block when Tito shouted, "Hold up a sec!"

Lenore mashed on the brakes, pitching forward. "What is it? What's wrong?"

"Gimme a sec!"

Twisting around in the driver's seat, Lenore saw Tito vanish out the broken side door. Ken scrambled out of his seat and snatched the bloody crowbar on the counter. Breathing heavily, looking far too pale, Ken guarded the door.

"Ken, take deep breaths. Don't hyperventilate," Grandma ordered in her strictest tone.

Forcing himself to obey, Ken dragged air past his trembling lips into his lungs.

Craning her neck, Lenore tried to see what Tito was up to. She spotted him darting up a narrow dirt driveway toward an abandoned dirt bike. At the end of the drive was an old ranch style house with the windows broken in their frames and the door ajar. She wasn't sure if it was abandoned or if it had come under the assault of zombies. The front yard was filled with discarded vehicles and appliances listing in the overgrown grass.

"What's that crazy Mexican doing?" Grandma muttered beside her.

"Hurry up, Tito!" Ken shouted. He was still shaking, but had a little more color in his face and no longer appeared on the verge of passing out.

Tito was almost to the dirt bike when two zombies rose out of the tall grass in the center of the yard. Their faces and necks were slathered in gore and they were both chewing.

Lenore began screaming just as grandma and Ken unleashed their own warning shouts, their voices mingling into a cacophony of incoherent words. Both zombies pivoted toward the RV before lurching into awkward lopes across the yard in the direction of the road instead of at Tito.

"Oh, shit! They're coming this way!" Ken gasped.

Tito took hold of the dirt bike's handlebars and yanked it upright. Casting a fearful glance toward the zombies, he began to run parallel to them, heading to the RV.

Realizing that prey was much closer than the big metal beast on the road, the two zombies altered their course. One was mangled and barely human in appearance. It dragged behind, one leg twisting as it tried to run. The other zombie's neck and shoulder was a ruin of flesh, but it was less mutilated and sprinted with terrifying sped at Tito.

"He's not going to make it!" Ken cried out in anguish.

"Come on!" Lenore screamed.

"Why'd he stop for that bike? Damn fool!" Grandma huffed. "Serves him right if he gets eaten."

"Grandma!" Lenore unbuckled her seatbelt. Grabbing the shotgun, she headed into the back. "Drive Grandma, but not until I tell you."

"You know they took my license!"

"It don't matter no more! Just drive when I tell you, Grandma!"

"Don't sass me!"

Lenore shoved Cher's carrier aside with her foot as she bolted down the short aisle. From the color of Ken's face, Lenore could tell he had forgotten to breathe again. She pushed him away from the doorway. Her stomach rolled when she saw how close the one zombie was to reaching her friend. The muscles and veins in Tito's neck and arms were straining as he ran alongside the dirt bike, pushing it with all his might.

Raising the shotgun, Lenore realized she could not get a clear shot with Tito running just ahead of the zombie.

"Dammit! Tito, I can't shoot him!"

Dropping the bike, Tito dashed to the RV. The zombie's feet tangled in the wheel of the bike as he tripped over it in his pursuit of Tito. With a growl, it fell forward, landing on its side as it twisted in the air. Lenore gasped as Tito yanked the shotgun out of her hands, swiveled about, and aimed at the zombie's head. The creature's head disintegrated into a mass of raw flesh as it tumbled.

The roar of the shotgun deafened Lenore and she ducked away, her hands flying to her ears. Stepping forward, Tito aimed toward the disgustingly-mangled zombie lurching across the lawn. The shot echoed around them and Lenore winced.

"There's more coming up the road!" Grandma was staring into her side mirror. "They're coming!"

Thrusting the shotgun into Lenore's hands, Tito ran for the bike.

"Are you crazy?" Lenore shouted after him. She again pushed Ken aside as she fumbled for the bag with the ammunition in it. Muttering, she struggled to get the zipper open.

"Get out of the way!" Tito's voice shouted.

Ken jumped aside just as a dirty bike wheel bounced over the doorstep. Tito shoved the bike into the narrow space, cursing in Spanish. His hair hung in his face, shiny and slick with sweat, as his dark eyes darted toward the road. Lenore knew that look. The damn zombies were coming and she was stuck at the back of the vehicle.

"Drive, Grandma, drive!" Tito called out, squeezing in beside the bike. He was dangerously close to the door and Ken thrust the crowbar at him. With a grateful nod, Tito snatched the weapon from his grasp.

The RV lurched forward as the old woman in the driver's seat struggled with the steering wheel. The gears squealed and the RV slowly rolled forward.

"Go, Grandma, go!" Lenore screamed.

"I know! I know!" Grandma shoved down on the accelerator.

"You have it in neutral!" Tito exclaimed. "Put it in drive!"

"I don't have my glasses! I can't see!"

Shoving aside the curtain over the back window, Lenore wished immediately she hadn't. A good size pack of mauled and bloody bodies, that should not be up and walking around, were rushing toward the RV.

"A crowbar ain't gonna do it," Lenore whispered.

"Reload the shotgun!" Ken shouted. "Do it."

"Grandma, get this thing going!" Tito ordered briskly, close to losing his temper. Lifting himself up and over the bike, using the counter as leverage, Tito dropped into the narrow space beside Lenore. He snatched the shotgun away from her then began to hastily rummage through the bag.

"Oh, hell!" Lenore heaved herself up and over the small dining area in the RV, half falling and climbing as she made her way to the front.

Ken picked up the crowbar and stood near the dirt bike jammed into the narrow space. It was blocking the open doorway, but it wouldn't be much protection if the swarm of undead reached them.

Looking over her shoulder, Lenore saw the first zombies reach the back of the RV. Their gory hands slapped against the window as they mashed their mauled faces against the glass.

"I can't get it to go!" Grandma screamed, shoving the accelerator down with one foot, the gear stuck firmly in neutral.

Lenore leaned forward, grabbed the stick, and shifted into drive.

The RV roared forward. Her grandmother gasped, but held onto the steering wheel. Lenore leaned over her to help steer.

"Just keep your foot down," Lenore instructed her grandmother.

"Off! Off! Off!" Ken screeched.

Lenore glanced over her shoulder to see a zombie clinging to the doorway and lashing out at Ken. Ken was swinging the crowbar at the creature while Tito struggled to get the shotgun loaded.

"Push the bike out! He'll fall!" Lenore instructed. Her throat was tight with fear and her heart hurt in her chest.

"No! Don't drop the bike!" Tito exclaimed.

Ken squealed as the female zombie snagged his crowbar with a hand that wasn't much more than bone and tendon. Her matted, bloody hair swung over a featureless face as she snarled. Pulling herself over the bike, using the crowbar as her line to Ken, her teeth snapped together.

"Let go of the crowbar!" Lenore released the steering wheel and rushed to help Ken.

Rising swiftly to his feet, Tito rammed the butt of the shotgun into the zombie's face, snapping her head back and throwing her off balance. Her fingers slipped from the doorway and she vanished from view as she tumbled onto the road.

Breathless, Lenore pulled Ken from the bike and doorway. "You should have shoved out the bike," Lenore chided Ken. He clung to her, shaking as he dragged deep breaths into his lungs.

"I told him not to," Tito said as he reloaded the shotgun.

"Why not?" Lenore demanded. "He could have died."

"Because I need it. As soon as we find a safe spot for you, I'm taking off," Tito said in a firm voice.

"Without you, we might die," Ken protested.

"No. I'll find you a safe place to hunker down. But I gotta find my family," Tito answered.

Ken fell into a nearby chair as Lenore moved toward the driver's seat. Her grandmother was silent, but she knew that the old woman was probably feeling much like she was.

Without Tito, they were all probably as good as dead.

18.
Losing The Knight In Shining Armor

The air outside was hot, humid, and heavy, but it was worse inside the RV. Tito, Lenore, and Ken were sweating profusely even with all the windows open. Even the breeze was hot. Grandma sat outside in a lawn chair, armed with her revolver, and watching out for any undead. Ken seriously doubted that any of the zombies would make it out into the middle of nowhere, which was their current location.

Tito had made Lenore drive for hours on back roads, farm roads, and dirt roads before finally settling on a location near the top of a hill with a good view of the surrounding area. There were trees for shade and shelter and a pond nearby that they could use for bathing, cooking and drinking. They'd have to boil the water before use, but it was better than nothing. They were miles away from the nearest highway with no towns within a thirty-mile radius.

Ken's heart pounded in his chest like the fierce beat of his favorite song. It really hurt and he wondered if he was having a heart attack. Forcing a deep breath into his lungs, he handed Tito another screw. His trembling hand gave his nerves away, but Tito didn't seem to notice.

Tito had snatched several pieces of wood off a lumber pile during their journey. Lenore held a thick L-shaped piece of wood in place next to the doorway as Tito used an electric drill to force the screw through the wood and wall, securing it. There were two brackets on the walls next to the door and one set in the middle of the door. Once their task was done, they would be able to brace the door using a two by four jammed into the four brackets. .

"Are you sure this will hold?" Lenore asked doubtfully.

"Yeah, I'm sure. But you shouldn't wait around if they come. Bar the door, gun the engine and take off."

"We're almost on fumes," Lenore reminded Tito.

"Yeah, I know. Go as far as you can. Hopefully, I'll be back with my family in a few days and it won't be no big deal," Tito answered. "I'll get gas then."

"What about that CB? Can you fix it?" Lenore asked.

Tito sighed, wagging his head sorrowfully. "I'm not good at electronics. Besides, it might be that we're out of range of anyone else. Or there ain't anyone else out there."

The grim expression on Tito's face did not comfort Ken in the least. Though no one dared speak it, the truth of the matter was that Tito's family was most likely dead. Ken didn't doubt Tito would return though. He had classified Tito as a *bad ass* in his mind. Not only was the short Latino seriously hot in a bad boy sort of way, but he was good at taking care of business.

Lenore gave Ken a dark look and he realized he was staring at Tito's back muscles straining under his shirt as he worked. Casting his gaze in the opposite direction from Tito's chiseled physique, Ken blushed. He had seriously gone way too long without a boyfriend.

"Okay, let's give this a try," Tito said, setting the drill on the counter. "Lenore, head outside, and when I tell you, push against the door."

With the short nod of her head, Lenore obeyed and Tito shut the door. Ken watched as Tito slid the wood brace across the door, shoving it between the three wood brackets.

"Okay, Lenore. Go for it!" Tito called out.

Even though Ken knew it was Lenore, he jumped when she hit the door. His already-racing heart sped up as she continued her assault. The door shuddered, but stayed secure.

"How hard are you hitting it?" Tito asked, leaning forward to watch the brackets.

"As hard as I can!" Lenore shouted from outside.

"Okay, stop." Tito leaned against the counter and sighed. "It's not going to hold for long, so you're going to have to keep that in mind. But at least it will buy you time."

Ken mopped the sweat from his brow with the bottom of his shirt. "Thanks, man. That's better than having the door flopping open."

Tito pulled the brace out of the brackets and the door swung open, revealing Lenore's sour expression. "Lenore, I'm heading out now. You got plenty of food, water, shelter and weapons. You should be okay. You guys hunker down and I'll be back soon."

Lenore scowled even more while Ken took a deep breath of hot, humid air, trying to steady his nerves.

"Good luck, Tito," Ken said at last.

Tito held out his hand and they shook hands. Ken wasn't sure if Tito's palm was sweaty from all his work, the heat, or his nerves. "Take care, Ken."

Lenore stepped away from the doorway to let Tito exit and Ken followed in his wake. Grandma slowly stood, her hand still clutching her weapon.

"I need to go find my family," Tito said to the old woman.

"I'll pray for you. I appreciate what you did for us today. You saved us," Grandma said, hugging him. "I'm so sorry about your mother."

Tito clung to the older woman for a long moment before letting go. "This is a shitty ass day, that's for damn sure."

"Don't get eaten," Lenore said in a somber voice.

Tito moved to hug her, saw her expression, thought better of it, and offered his hand. Lenore shook it briefly, then handed him the bag of shotgun ammo and the shotgun.

"You better take this," Lenore said crisply.

"You might need it," Tito said, reaching out for the weapon and bag, but looking unsure.

"You're going where there are a lot more zombies than here. And you're coming back, right?"

Tito nodded solemnly, his hand closing on the weapon. "Yeah. We'll be back."

"Then take it. We got Grandma's revolver and some ammunition for it."

Tito slung the bag over his shoulder and held the shotgun in his hands almost reverently. "Thanks for this."

"Just don't die." Lenore folded her arms over her bosom and glared at him.

"I won't. And you take of yourselves," Tito said, shifting on his feet, his eyes hidden by his sunglasses.

Ken could have been reading him wrong, but Tito appeared to be uncomfortable with leaving them behind. The other man hesitated for a second before walking over to the motor bike he had snagged earlier. Strapping the bag to the bike and figuring out how to secure the rifle, Tito's face set into a look of sheer determination. He straddled the bike and without another word, he gunned the engine and roared down the hill, plumes of dirt tossed up behind the wheels. Ken watched as the hot wind caught the dust and sent it swirling across the ground like mini-tornados. He listened to the fading sound of the motorbike with a heavy heart.

"Chances are he ain't coming back even if he does find his family," Ken decided, depression settling over him like a thick mantle. Why would Tito come back to an old woman, a chubby grumpy girl and a flaming fag?

"No. Tito's a man of his word. If he finds his family or if he doesn't, he'll come back," Grandma decided, fanning herself with her hand. "Too hot to be outdoors anymore. I'm going in to sit a spell inside."

"You really think he'll come back?" Ken asked hopefully. He just couldn't imagine continuing to survive without someone like Tito helping them.

"If he can," Grandma assured him before climbing into the RV.

Lenore pursed her lips, glowering into the valley below. "I wouldn't count on it," she said after a beat.

Sighing, Ken followed Grandma into the warm RV. Cher was still in her carrier, but sleeping peacefully. He snagged a bottle of water from the well-stocked cabinets (thank you, Mr. Thames), before sitting at the small dining table. He wished they could run the air conditioner, but they were plain lucky they had had enough fuel to make it out this far. The luxuries of life were gone now.

Folding his arms on the table, he rested his head on his forearms. He wondered how long they would have to wait for Tito to return.

19.
Death Comes Again

--Six Weeks Later

The storms the night before had battered the small RV, but now that the morning had come, there was a cool breeze wafting through the tiny home. Ken rolled carefully out of his bed above the cab and dropped to the floor. Lenore was still asleep and snoring in the top bunk bed in the rear of the vehicle. Cher yawned on the dashboard of the RV, stretched, then went back to sleep.

Ken rubbed his eyes as he stumbled into the small kitchen. Their food supplies were dwindling, but Grandma had made some pancakes using the makeshift stove they had rigged over a campfire. The old woman always woke very early to make breakfast and instant coffee so she could sit outside and watch the sun rise. Grandma made the small RV feel like a home instead of a prison.

As usual, his nightmares were full of the rabid undead and his heart still beat harshly in his chest. He hated waking up from bad dreams. Since they had escaped into the hills, he couldn't sleep without bone-chilling visions of the undead invading his mind.

Ken glanced out the open entrance to see the sun was just peeking over the hills. No matter how lovely the countryside was in the spring, he missed his old apartment. He missed civilization. He missed everything about the old world. He still couldn't believe it was almost two months since they had taken refuge in the hills.

Stacking pancakes on a plastic plate, Ken sighed. It was difficult not to fall prey to the depression that devoured him if he obsessed about the precariousness of their situation. Even though zombies had not appeared in their area, he was certain the undead were still out there. What little reception the radio had the first few days after their escape had revealed a world in its death throes. After a week all that remained was static. Finally, they had turned it off.

With a sigh, Ken shook off the negative thoughts threatening to overwhelm him. Grandma always said to be happy for another day of life. He needed to remember her words when he felt this way.

Ken snagged a fork and headed outside to enjoy his morning meal. The old woman was seated in a plastic lawn chair facing the sunrise, her gray hair ruffled by the morning breeze. Ken plopped into the chair next to her and shoved the first bite of pancake into his mouth.

"Pretty day, huh?" he said.

It really was beautiful. The horizon was painted with pink, lavender and gold. The indigo of the night sky was fading to a clear blue.

Grandma didn't answer.

"Grandma?"

Ken cocked his head to peer at the older woman. Her eyes were closed and her mouth was slightly open. "Hey, Grandma?"

The old woman remained eerily still. Gradually, Ken realized that her chest was not rising and falling with breath.

"Grandma?"

Afraid, Ken reached out and touched her hand. It felt cool to his touch.

"Grandma!"

Scrambling to his feet, he knocked his breakfast onto the ground. He grabbed the older woman by the shoulders and shook her.

"Grandma, please wake up! Please wake up!"

Lenore stumbled out of the RV. "What are you shouting about?"

"It's Grandma! I don't think she's breathing!" Ken exclaimed.

Lenore's forehead creased as she hurried over.

His fingers slid over the old woman's wrist, searching for a pulse. He was trembling with emotion and felt like throwing up.

"Grandma?" Lenore leaned over and cupped her hand over the old woman's mouth and nose. Resting her cheek against the woman's soft white hair, Lenore squeezed her eyes shut. "Grandma..."

Ken fumbled with the old woman's neck, trying to find a pulse of life. His thoughts swirled in a panic as he realized he had never learned CPR.

Lenore sat heavily on the ground, silent tears streaming down her face. Her thick fingers closed over her grandmother's wrist as she leaned her forehead against the old woman's knee. "She's not here no more, Ken."

Ken touched the old woman's face lightly, his hand covering her mouth, emulating what Lenore had done. He was terrified that she would suddenly snarl and bite off his fingers, but he had to make sure she really wasn't breathing.

"She's gone, Ken!" Lenore shouted. "She ran out of her pills and she told me she was having chest pains. She's gone!"

Slumping to the ground, Ken felt tears welling. Cher wandered over, flicking her calico tail, regarding them with interest. "What if she comes back?"

"She won't. She didn't get bit. That was what the radio said does it. The damn bite," Lenore grumbled, her face contorted with emotion. "She ain't coming back. She's gone for good."

As Cher curled around him, purring loudly, Ken stared at the old woman he had come to love so dearly. Now all that remained was him, Lenore and Cher. Tito and Grandma were gone.

"We're going to have to bury her," Lenore said at last, her voice rough.

"Then what?" Ken asked.

Lenore shrugged.

Ken rubbed Cher's thick coat as he glanced toward the rising sun. Usually the sunrise filled him with hope, but today, it filled him with dread.

20.
What To Do Next?

Caked in mud, Lenore sat next to her grandmother's grave and stared at the sunset. It had taken her and Ken all day to dig the grave. They had only one shovel, so Ken had grabbed a steel pot. On his knees, he had helped her all day long, sweat and tears mingling on both their faces. They only took breaks to go out into the trees to relieve themselves and to eat a cold meal of ravioli.

Now it was done, and Lenore sat in silence between her grandmother and Ken. The storms the night before had made their job easier by soaking the ground with rain, but now the humidity and mud made Lenore feel even more surly than usual.

In her hand were the hairpins her grandmother always wore in her hair. Lenore had carefully pulled them out of her grandmother's bun and arranged her hair like a halo around her head. It bothered Lenore that they had to bury her without a coffin. A bed sheet had been her burial shroud. Yet that was a much better fate than most of the world had suffered.

Cher stretched out on top of the fresh grave and yawned. The calico usually kept close to the RV, afraid of the great outdoors. Ken had kept her inside his home her whole life and the cat would flee to the RV at the slightest sound. One of her favorite spots was Grandma's lap. Seeing the cat resting on her grandmother's grave was strangely comforting.

"What are we going to do now?" Ken asked in a sorrowful tone.

All day he had been asking the exact same question, and Lenore never had an answer for him. Their food supply was diminishing and they had barely any gas in the tank. Maybe it had been foolish to stay put, waiting in vain for Tito to return, but Lenore and Ken had truly believed he would make it back. Now it was clear he wasn't going to and her grandmother was gone.

"I think it's time for us to move on," Lenore said at last. She didn't want to die. For a while she had convinced herself that staying put was the way to survive, but now she wasn't too sure.

"Where will we go?"

"Hell if I know."

Getting to her feet, Lenore walked to the RV. Cher's cry of protest behind her informed her that Ken was following in her wake clutching his cat. Stepping into the RV, she lit a candle and set it on the table. Ken followed her in, set Cher on the bench and shut the door.

Lenore retrieved a map from the glove compartment. Spreading it out on the table, she studied their location. Tito had marked it with a small X before he had left. Ken slid into the booth and pet Cher while Lenore hunched over the map.

"Should we go to a big city?" Ken wondered. "Or to Fort Hood? Wouldn't there be lots of soldiers there with big guns?"

"Lots of zombies, too," Lenore mumbled. "Nearest town is Ashley Oaks."

"Can we make it there?" Ken peered at the point on the map where her dirt-encrusted finger pointed.

"Not sure. We could try to go the other way to Emorton, but I think it's too far out. We might make it part of the way to Ashley Oaks. Then we'd have to walk the rest of the way."

"Walk?" Ken's voice cracked with fear.

Lenore's stomach was roiling with the mere thought of being out in the elements, but she didn't know what else to do. "Well, we stay here and starve, or we try to go get help. Maybe we'll find another car or a gas station before we run out of gas."

Ken tapped his fingers on the table in a nervous staccato. "I don't want to get eaten, Lenore."

"Me neither. I like my parts where they are. I don't want to be a zombie barbecue. But we can't stay here. We need to go before it gets any worse for us." Lenore scanned the interior of the small mobile home. "So what do we have in here we can use to help ourselves?"

"Revolver, a crowbar, a knife, and a frying pan," Ken said. ticking off each item on his fingers. "We also have a CB that doesn't work."

"Tito said we're out of range up here," Lenore reminded her friend. A thought slowly formed into an idea. "We could maybe try to get into range. Call out for help. There has gotta be people still out there alive. This is Texas."

"Yeah, the rednecks are probably doing great!" Ken's grin pushed the fear out of his eyes. "We can call for help. Maybe the military will find us!"

Frowning, Lenore's tired mind attempted to formulate a plan of action. It felt good to be at least thinking about doing something other than sitting around waiting for either Tito to miraculously appear or for the zombies to find them.

"How much ammunition do we have?" Lenore asked.

"Enough to kill eighteen zombies if we hit them in the head the first time," Ken answered honestly.

"Then we better hit them in the head the first time." Lenore tried to measure on the map with her fingers, estimating the distance to Ashley Oaks. They were definitely going to run out of gas on their way. "You ever been to Ashley Oaks?"

"Uh, yeah. The stupid ex would take me there for their Peach Cobbler festival. It was like this huge deal in that town." Ken kissed the top of Cher's head and cuddled the cat.

"Think anyone there might be alive?" Lenore wiped the sticky, dirty sweat from her forehead and rubbed her hand on her jeans.

Ken answered with a shrug.

"Do you remember there being any gas stations or anything like that?"

"Uh, no. But I don't pay attention to that stuff. I usually read in the car."

It would be a huge risk, but all that was left to eat of the food they had brought with them and Mr. Thames's camping wares was pancakes and a few cans of soup and ravioli. Could they really just sit here and die? Neither one of them knew how to hunt or grow food. Lenore just couldn't see what else they could do. Guilt ate at her as she wondered if she could have saved her grandmother's life if they had tried to leave earlier.

Of course, they could be leaving the safety of their isolated haven to die somewhere out in the world of the dead. Lenore shivered.

"Are you sure we should do this?" Ken asked in a soft voice. He had been staring at her face, probably reading her thoughts. She hated it when he was so insightful.

"We probably should have done this earlier," Lenore groused. "But we kept waiting on Tito. And Grandma seemed happy up here."

"And we were too scared to leave," Ken added.

"Uh huh."

"I'm still too scared to leave." Ken gave Cher several long kisses on top of her head. The tears in his eyes caught the candlelight.

"We can always just sit here and wait to die," Lenore said with a shrug. The idea sickened her. She didn't want to starve to death. Or get eaten. "We're damned if we do, damned if we don't."

"Can we think about it a few more days?"

Lenore nodded. "We got enough food for a little bit longer." Looking out the window at the pond, Lenore sighed. "I'm going to clean up."

"I'll come with you."

They gathered clean clothes and towels. Leaving Cher safely inside, they walked down to the pond. Their flashlights illuminated the tall grass and few trees. Lenore didn't particularly like the dark, but she couldn't stand to be dirty.

Under the full moon they washed up, changed into fresh clothing, and washed their dirty outfits. The world around them was peaceful and Lenore wondered if she was being rash. Maybe she just wanted to run away because her grandmother was gone. The emptiness inside of her was crushing.

Carefully, she withdrew her grandmother's hairpins from her jeans. Her hair was grown out and ratty. It annoyed her, but she didn't have anything to secure it until now. Tears blinded her eyes as she carefully French-braided her hair back from her face, slipping the hairpins into the woven hair to hold the style. When she finished, she rested her hands against her hair, remembering her grandmother's gentle touch.

In silence they trudged up to the RV. Ken hung their wet clothes on the makeshift clothesline they had strung on the branches of a tree. While he was doing that, Lenore poured the tepid water they had boiled earlier over the campfire into a gallon jug. She hoped there was some Kool-Aid and sugar left. She hated the taste of the pond water even after it had been boiled to rid it of impurities.

Lenore kicked dirt onto the fire to extinguish it. Turning, she saw Ken draping his jeans over the line. A shadowy figure lurked just beyond him, moving slowly through the brush.

"Ken!" Lenore shouted.

He jerked about, staring at her in confusion.

"Run!"

Panicking, Ken ran in her direction and away from the RV. Lenore pointed at the RV, breaking into a run.

"No! That way!"

Skidding around, Ken retreated to the RV. He was almost to the entry when the zombie lurched out from the gloom under the trees and into the moonlight. With a screech, Ken dashed past it and dove into the vehicle.

"Get the gun!" Lenore screamed stumbling to a halt. The zombie was between her and safety. She cursed herself for becoming so lax in their security. It had felt so safe up here they had stopped carrying the revolver after the first week and a half. The beam of her flashlight caught the zombie in its light as it lurched after Ken.

For a moment she was terrified it was her grandmother risen from the grave, but then she saw it was a man wearing bloodstained coveralls. The creature twisted around on its skinny legs toward her, abandoning its pursuit of Ken. Lenore swung the heavy gallon jug at the zombie's head as it lunged. The impact shattered the plastic and sent warm water over both of them. The blow was violent enough to knock the zombie backward. It reeled, trying to regain its balance.

Lenore surged toward the dark gaping entry to the RV. The light from her flashlight swung crazily over the ground as she pounded up the incline. Her lungs gasped for air and she felt light-headed. After all the hard work they had done today, she was physically exhausted.

The reek of the zombie filled her nose as she pounded past it. Hurtling through the doorway, she almost knocked Ken over. Clutching the revolver, Ken screamed in terror.

Lenore scrambled to shut the door, but Ken shoved her aside and aimed at the undead man. The explosive sound of the shots nearly deafened Lenore. She flinched as the revolver roared. Ken fired all six shots and the gun clicked empty. The zombie lay on the ground moaning, one leg shattered and an arm hanging from sinews. Lenore grabbed the door, swung it shut, and barred it.

"You idiot!"

Ken staggered away from her, hyperventilating. Cher was somewhere in the RV hissing angrily. Collapsing against the kitchen counter, Ken shook violently.

Despite her anger, Lenore understood his terror. She gently tugged the revolver out of his hands and set it aside.

"Ken," she said in a low voice.

Shivering, he stared at her through glassy eyes.

"Go lay down."

Ken nodded and wobbled to the rear of the RV.

Sighing, Lenore pulled the crowbar off the counter. For a few minutes she checked outside with her flashlight, peering into the darkness. No more shambling shapes emerged from the darkness. Only the one zombie keened as it tried to crawl to the RV.

Clenching the crowbar in her hands, she unbarred the door and stepped outside.

It took two whacks to kill the zombie. Once done, she wiped the end of the crowbar off on the grass. The wind whistled through the tree branches and stirred the tall grass.

All seemed calm once again.

As Lenore climbed back into the RV and secured the door, she wondered how long it would last.

21.
Time to Go

Curled up on the bottom bunk, Ken wished he could stop crying. Though he managed to stifle his sobs, he was sure Lenore heard him. She had climbed onto the top bunk after going outside and killing the zombie. He had expected her to yell and call him names after he had been such an idiot by wasting six bullets. Instead, she had been silent, which had been in its own way even worse. She was Eeyore to his Tigger, and when she was grumpy at him he knew everything was okay between them.

Silence scared him.

Cher nudged his nose with hers before crawling over him to settle into the small of his back. Her presence was a comfort. He could always depend on her love. Maybe he was being foolish, but he wondered if Lenore hated him now. He was such a stupid Nancy girl. He couldn't even deal with one zombie.

But then again, he had avoided confrontations his whole life. Anxiety attacks had plagued him all through his formative years. It was very hard for him to stand up for himself or involve himself in any physical confrontation. He had never hit anyone in his entire life even when he was being beat up.

Last night, his desire had been to run into the RV and hide, but the thought of losing Lenore, his best friend -- only friend now -- had compelled him to take action. Of course, that had resulted in him wasting ammo and not even killing the zombie.

Sniffling, he curled up on the pillow. Sleep felt far away. His senses were heightened, his ears straining to hear every sound. The creaking of a tree branch sent shivers down his spine. The wind swirling through the field and the noises of the night creatures sounded eerie tonight. Of course, what he was truly straining to hear was the low, terrible moans of the undead.

It was warm in the RV. The windows were cracked open just enough to let a breeze in, but it was still humid and he felt sticky. He wished he could fall asleep and forget the horrible day, but he felt painfully-awake. Worried that the zombies could be creeping up on the RV, he slid out of bed.

A quick glance out of each window, including the windshield, reassured him that no more of the shambling dead had reached their safe haven. The moonlight illuminated the mesquite tree that sheltered Grandma's grave. His overzealous mind began to ponder the possibility of the old woman crawling out of her grave as a ravenous zombie. Shivering, he tried to dispel that frightening notion and returned to bed.

Cher glared at him as he jostled her and made a great fuss over having to resettle herself into a new position. He felt fresh tears fill his eyes at the thought of his little kitty girl suffering alongside him through this nightmare. He had noticed she had lost a little weight and it saddened him. Cher and Lenore were all he had left in the world.

If Lenore wasn't mad at him...

Changing positions every few minutes, he tried to find a comfortable spot in the bed. He grumpily kept adjusting the pillow until Cher had enough and stalked off in a huff to sleep somewhere else. He considered sleeping in his regular bunk, but he wanted to be close to Lenore even if she was mad at him. If only he could get comfortable...

Trying to fall asleep became a nightmare. Ken counted sheep, counted backward, tried to pretend he was floating on a cloud, and a variety of other mind tricks all in an effort to fool himself into sleeping. He finally gave up, convinced he was doomed to a long sleepless night, when sunlight struck his eyes, waking him. Groggily, he pulled himself upright, surprised that he had actually slumbered. He must have been dreaming he was still awake.

Standing, he checked Lenore's bunk to see that she was gone. A sour little knot of anxiety clenched inside of him as he hurried through the small RV looking for her and his cat. Cher was asleep in a sunbeam on the dashboard, but Lenore was nowhere to be found. The door was slightly ajar and he tentatively shoved it open. Lenore stood before the smoldering campfire gazing toward the meadows below. The revolver was clutched in one of her hands. The corpse of the zombie was nowhere to be seen and Ken shivered at the memory of the creature.

"The zombie..." Ken started, then faltered. He had left Lenore to deal with the zombie alone last night and with its body this morning. He felt like a jerk.

"Dragged him off into the woods," Lenore answered. "But I'm not worried about him no more. I'm worried about them."

Ken staggered forward, blinking his eyes rapidly as they adjusted to the brightness of the day.

Wading through the high, dry grass toward the encampment were five zombies. The wind stole their moans away, but he could see their open mouths as their hands slashed at the air.

"Shit," Ken gasped.

"Time to go," Lenore said grimly.

"They have terrible timing," Ken groused.

"Grandma would say it was a sign from God. That it's time for us to step out in faith," Lenore answered.

"You think so?"

Lenore's solemn expression made his heart hurt for her. The pain in her eyes was painfully-evident. Finally, she nodded. "Yeah. If they had showed up earlier, they might have gotten Grandma, or us. But she's with the Lord now and we're left to fend for ourselves. We're younger and stronger than she was. She got to spend some quiet days out here. I don't think we're gonna get those quiet days."

Tears in his eyes again, Ken embraced Lenore, holding her tight whether she wanted to be or not. To his surprise, she didn't fight him off, but rested her head on his shoulder.

"I'm sorry I wimped out last night," he whispered.

"You tried to save me," Lenore answered. "That's not being a wimp. Now you can't shoot worth shit, but at least you tried."

"I'll let you handle the gun," Ken said with a sigh. Releasing her, Ken started to collect their things. Lenore had boiled more water and had poured it into a different container since she had ruined the other one last night. He snagged that and the campfire stove. "How long do we have before they get here?"

"Thirty minutes I bet. Let's not be here when they arrive."

"Where are we going?" He knew he sounded like a broken record, but he was at a loss as to how to handle any of this. Lenore was much stronger than he was and he knew it.

"Away from here," Lenore answered with a shrug. "As Grandma used to say, 'The Lord will lead.'"

"And if He doesn't?"

"We'll make it up as we go."

Casting a worried glance at the zombies, Ken realized that was the best answer he was going to get.

22.
Nothing Is Easy

Lenore shoved the lawn chairs into the compartment in the back of the RV and wiped her palms off on her jeans. The day was cool, but she was sweating more from nerves than exertion.

"C'mere, Cher!" Ken wailed again from outside.

Lenore's pocket was full of bullets and the gun was tucked into the pocket of her hoodie. She glanced out the window, checking on the progress of the zombies. They were circumventing the pond and slogging along the muddy bank. Another ten minutes and they would be upon them.

"Cher! Stop being difficult!" Ken's voice was starting to sound hysterical.

The cat rarely went outside, but she had suddenly sprinted out the door just as they were finishing packing the vehicle.

"Ken!"

"I'm trying to get her! I can't leave her! Cher, bad cat! Bad! C'mere!"

Lenore sighed and headed out the door to help him. Ken sprawled on his stomach, trying to reach the cat under the RV. Grumbling, Lenore sank to her knees and peered under the vehicle. Cher was sitting directly out of reach, languorously cleaning one foot.

"Really? Really? You pick this damn time to take a bath?" Lenore groused at the cat.

Cher flicked a dismissive look at Lenore.

"Ken, we might have to leave her," Lenore said, hating to say the words. She looked over her shoulder, checking on the zombies' progress. They were out of her line of sight, below the crest of the hill.

"No, I can't!" Ken glared at Lenore, then tried to stealthily edge up a few more inches.

The cat gave him a sharp look, her muscles tensing. Lenore was certain the cat was about to bolt.

A low, hungry moan floated on the wind.

Cher lifted her head higher, staring past the humans with bright intense eyes. Ears slightly flicking forward, she lowered the foot she had been cleaning.

"Ken," Lenore whispered. She could barely see the top of a zombie's head peeking over the hill's slope.

"Cher, come to daddy. The bad things are coming. Come here." The tone in Ken's voice was heartbreaking. It was desperation mixed with love.

Shoving up with her hands, Lenore scrambled to her feet. Her fingers closed over the revolver in her pocket. She stared at the zombie staggering fully into view a little more than fifty feet away. Lifting its hands, the creature let out a horrible cry.

"Ken!"

"Got her! I got her!" Ken exclaimed. "Help me up!"

Lenore leaned over, grabbed the waistband of his jeans, and dragged him out from under the RV. Twisting around, Ken scrambled to his feet clutching Cher in his arms. She was clinging to his shirt, claws dug in, staring at the zombie with wide, frightened eyes.

The zombie was now moving faster, spurred on by the sight of living human flesh.

"Get in now," Lenore ordered as she drew the firearm.

Skirting around her, Ken hopped through the entrance. Lenore followed, her eyes still on the zombie. She quickly pulled the door shut and grabbed the two by four. Shoving the wood into place, she felt her heart beating ever faster. The groan of the zombie sent shivers down her spine. The answering moans of the other undead creatures in its wake made her breath catch. Her hand was shaking as she tucked the revolver back into her hoodie.

"Keep it together, girl," she mumbled.

She hurried to the driver's seat, brushing past Ken who was shoving a hissing Cher into her carrier. Lenore slid into the driver's seat and glanced out the window to see the zombie stumbling around the campfire, growling.

"Lenore!" Ken cried out.

"I see it," Lenore answered.

After fastening her seatbelt and making sure she could reach the revolver in her pocket without hindrance, Lenore meticulously followed Tito's instructions on how to start the vehicle. She closed her eyes in prayer.

"Dear Jesus, let this work," she breathed.

"You do remember how to hotwire it?"

"Shut up, Ken."

The engine gave a little cough, but sputtered out.

"What's happening?" Ken gasped.

"Low on gas and it's been sitting for a month," Lenore answered tersely. "Give me a second."

The sound of something impacting with the RV made both of them start. A quick peek at the rearview mirror made Lenore shudder. The zombie was slamming its fists against the side of the vehicle.

"Lenore..."

"Shhh..." Lenore tried again and lightly pumped the gas.

The engine briefly came to life, then died.

Ken shrieked as the zombie reached his window. It beat its putrid, rotting hands against the glass, hissing.

Lenore again tried to spark the engine to life.

The engine weakly roared and Lenore pushed down on the accelerator, giving it more precious gas. In her periphery the zombie assaulted the window, growling as Ken cringed away chanting her name like a prayer.

"Got it," Lenore said, then shoved the vehicle into gear.

The RV lurched into motion and rolled forward. The zombie's bloody hands slid off the window as it struggled to keep up with the vehicle. Lenore turned onto the narrow drive that would lead to a farm road. The wheels slipped on the gravel, stalling the RV for a second, before they regained traction. Lenore clutched the wheel tightly as the RV bounced over the rutted road.

Ken leaned his forehead on the dashboard, dragging air into his lungs. "Oh, my God! Did you see its face? It was all torn up. I don't even know if it was a man or woman."

"It don't matter, Ken. It's dead."

Lenore flicked her gaze to the side mirror again and was relieved to see the zombies were out of view. Her stomach was doing acrobatics. Cher was meowing in her carrier and Lenore didn't blame her. The mere sight of the walking dead was enough to make her want to scream. They had spent so much time on the hilltop safe and far away from the rest of the dying world she had forgotten how horrible they looked. It was worse than any movie and the smell was nearly unbearable.

Settling in his seat, Ken took a deep breath. "I was so scared the engine wouldn't start."

"But it did start," Lenore answered briskly. "Don't go freaking out after we've gotten away."

Ken frowned at her. "I'm not freaking out."

"Uh huh."

"No. I'm fine. I'm the epitome of fine. It was just so damn ugly! And...scary...and...the engine wasn't behaving and..."

"Freaking. Out."

Ken pouted. "Fine. Maybe just a little."

"Get the map and guide me. Also, turn on that CB. See if we can pick something up."

Unbuckling himself, Ken stuck his tongue before disappearing to do as she asked.

Lenore watched the sides of the road for any signs of the zombies. The junipers, cedars, and oaks lining the road could be hiding anything from zombies to deer. The last thing they needed to do was hit something on the road. Being stranded in an area where zombies were prowling around was not a situation she wanted to experience.

The trees gave way to brush, the road flattening out between two large fields. The fences were still intact, and Lenore felt a little safer as she drove.

Ken returned to his seat with the map and flipped on the CB. Static filled the air, competing with Cher's questioning meows.

"I highlighted the path we should take," Lenore said to Ken. "Just tell me what to do once we hit the farm road."

"Okay."

"And start flipping channels on that thing," Lenore ordered, briskly indicating the CB with one hand.

Ken nodded and started to dial through the various channels. There was only static and silence. Ken turned up the sound and listened intently.

"There has to be someone out there, right?"

"Not if everyone is dead," Lenore answered.

"Maybe we're not in range yet." Ken's face wrinkled with worry as he continued to skip through the channels.

Cher finally ceased yowling, much to Lenore's relief. Casting her gaze back and forth between the two sides of the road, she was relieved to see nothing stirring in the overgrown fields.

"Where do you think those zombies came from?" Ken asked.

Lenore shrugged. "I wouldn't know. Maybe from a farm. Or a road. A town. It's been a month and a half. They could have just been walking, looking for someone to eat." The engine was starting to pull uncomfortably and Lenore studied the gas gage. It was technically on empty. Did that mean they had a few more gallons or was this morning about to turn really sour?

The static hissed and whined as Ken continued to turn the dial.

"Do you think they can smell us or something?"

Lenore snorted. "From miles away? I think they just got lucky."

"I guess. I'm just glad they didn't show up when..." He faltered. "We really dropped our guard."

"Yeah. We ain't doing that again." Lenore pressed on the accelerator a little harder, feeling it starting to resist. They were going to need a miracle and fast.

A voice sizzled out of the static just before Ken flipped to another channel.

"Go back!"

"Did you hear it?" Ken squealed.

"Go back!"

Fingers shaking, Ken carefully turned the dial backward, both of them listening intently.

"...run was pretty successful. We're heading back now," a man's voice said.

"Things are clear here, so just head to the gate," a woman's voice answered.

"What do I do?" Ken gasped.

"Call them, idiot!" Lenore snatched the mouthpiece off the dash and tossed it to him. The engine was feeling even more sluggish now. She fervently whispered prayers in her mind.

Pressing down the button, Ken said, "Uh, hello?"

"What was that, Ed?" the woman's voice asked.

"I didn't say nothin', Peggy," Ed answered.

"Uh, hi. I'm Ken. Who are you? Hi," Ken said.

Lenore hit him.

"What?"

Lenore glowered.

"Hey, there, Ken," the woman's voice said pleasantly enough. "I don't think we've talked before. Where you calling from?"

"An RV."

Lenore hit him again.

"An RV? Y'all are out there driving around?"

"We were camping, but Grandma died and then zombies showed up and--oww!" Ken rubbed his arm. "What?"

"Find out where they are!" Lenore shouted at him.

"You okay, Ken?"

"Yeah. I just...yeah. I'm fine. So, me and my best friend are out here and there are zombies." Ken flattened himself against the door trying to avoid Lenore's fist.

"My name is Peggy and I'm the city secretary here in Ashley Oaks. You looking for a place to hole up?"

"Yeah. We're low on gas and food and I think there are more zombies..." Ken's voice faded out.

Lenore slowed the RV as the farm road came into view. The brake felt hard under her foot. They were running out of time. Then her heart nearly came to a stop as she saw what awaited them on the road.

"Ken?" the woman's voice said through the white noise of the CB.

"Uh, there are zombies," Ken said in a frightened voice. "A lot of them."

A crowd of zombies shambled along the road toward them. As the RV neared the turnoff, the zombie moans swelled in anticipation.

"Where are you?" Peggy asked, her voice calm, but urgent.

Ken fumbled with the map. "Uh, uh...farm road 1226. It's on the way to Emorton."

"Are you close to Emorton?"

"No, uh, we're near some farm. I can see the house from here."

Lenore turned onto the farm road, the steering wheel fighting her.

"A big blue and white house with a red barn?"

"Yeah," Ken answered, his gaze riveted to the zombie mass in the rearview mirror.

"Okay, this is how you get to where we are..." Peggy started to ramble off directions, but Lenore had stopped listening.

The engine sputtered and died.

"Ask them if they can come get us," Lenore said sourly as Ken's eyes widened.

Three hundred yards behind the RV, the zombies moaned hungrily.

23.
Parade of the Dead

Ken felt like someone had punched him in the chest. He couldn't breathe and he was sure his heart had stopped. Cher started yowling again and the nice lady on the CB was saying something, but nothing registered in his brain but the moans of the dead that were stumbling toward the stalled RV.

They were going to die.

Lenore snatched the mouthpiece out of his hand. "We're out of gas and time. There is a bunch of them heading our way."

In shock, Ken turned and stared at his cat in her carrier. She was hissing and growling, her back arched and her fur on end.

"Slow ones. Real slow. There is no way the RV is gonna hold up though. We got a busted door," Lenore's voice answered the woman's questions.

Her words gradually sunk through the numbness encompassing Ken's mind. Sliding off his seat, he tottered to the counter where the crowbar lay. He picked it up and grabbed Cher's carrier. The weight in his hands drew him slowly out of his fog into reality.

Lenore hauled herself out of the driver's seat. Her chubby face set with grim determination, she hurried past Ken, snatching up a hunting knife and shoving it into her hoodie pocket. Out the back window Ken could see the zombies gaining on the RV.

"What are we going to do?" Ken whispered, forcing words out of his constricted throat. His voice quivered with his distress.

"Start walking," Lenore answered. Her voice was low and tense.

"We can't! They'll...they'll..." Ken felt tears in his eyes. He thought of Mr. Cloy and the dead town they had escaped. He didn't want to die like that.

"We can, Ken. Those bastards are slow. We can outpace them. We just need to stay ahead of them. That lady on the CB is sending people to save us. We gotta move." Lenore searched around for anything else she could use as a weapon.

Ken couldn't stop staring at the mass of mutilated and gore covered people marching toward the RV. "Can't we just hide in here?"

"That door is gonna give out," Lenore said, pointing to the side door. "We'll be *dead* by the time those people get here." She cast one long look out the back window, scrutinizing the crowd. "They're slow. See?"

"But...but..." Ken faltered as Lenore gave him a dark look. then brushed past him.

She didn't take the side door, but crawled over the passenger seat instead. Ken followed, his legs wobbly and unsure. Cher hissed angrily, her weight shifting constantly in the carrier. Handing the carrier to Lenore, Ken slid over the seat. His feet dangling out of the RV, he froze. He could *smell* the dead. They were that close.

"Ken, move it," Lenore ordered.

"I can't!" Ken wailed. Panicking, he grabbed for the carrier. He and Cher would hide inside. It would be safer than walking ahead of a zombie parade.

Lenore swung the cat out of his reach and snagged his wrist. With one swift jerk, she hauled him out of the RV. His feet twisted under him as he landed on the hot asphalt, and he fell to his knees. Tiny pebbles bit into his hands and knees. Looking up, he saw the dead were even closer. Their moans were growing in volume at the sight of the living flesh.

Another hard yank drew him to his feet. Lenore dragged him along as she set a quick pace away from the RV and the horde of undead. "C'mon, Ken. Keep moving. I don't want to die today."

Ken struggled to make his feet and legs work. He kept tripping and stumbling as the slap of many feet against the asphalt mingled with the constant groans of the zombies.

"Don't look behind us," Lenore commanded sternly. "Just keep walking."

"I don't want to die," Ken wailed.

"Then keep walking." Lenore glanced behind them, but her dark eyes did not betray any emotion other than agitation.

After a few minutes he got his limbs to start working correctly and found the rhythm that matched Lenore's steady pace. She handed him Cher. The cat hissed and growled angrily.

Lenore stole another look behind them. She lifted one eyebrow.

"What is it?" Ken asked, not daring to take a peek.

"Some of them must have thought there are people in the RV. They already have the side door open," Lenore answered.

Ken felt his bowels churn as he envisioned himself trapped with Cher inside the RV. "Thank you, Lenore," he whispered, chastened by his earlier behavior.

"I ain't going to let you die," Lenore vowed. "So keep walking. They're following, but we got some distance now."

The sun blazed hot as it continued its ascent across the blue morning sky. The asphalt grew warmer beneath their feet and the sun's rays burned against his head and shoulders. Sweat trickled down his face and rolled between his shoulder blades. Lenore's face was dotted with beads of sweat. He knew she was fit for her size and her pace was brisk.

The zombie moans echoed through the Texas Hill Country. The RV had stalled on a flat stretch, but the road was slowly curving upward. Ken started to feel the burn in his calves and he wished he had kept up some sort of exercise routine when they had been in hiding. Lenore kept her strides quick and sure, occasionally glancing behind her.

Ken dared to look.

The zombies were not faltering in their pursuit. Their twisted forms jerked strangely as they followed on mutilated and broken legs. A few were limping badly and straggled along at the back of the pack. Their faces and exposed skin were darkened from exposure and their tattered clothes were covered in dried blood. Broken and stained teeth gnashed in torn faces. Claw-like hands dug at the air as if the creatures were trying to scrabble their way to Ken and Lenore. They were between seventy-five and a hundred yards back, but the distance felt miniscule.

Now he understood what it meant to be so scared you felt like you were going to shit your pants. Never had he wanted to go to the toilet so bad. His intestines were cramping and he felt sick to his stomach.

Lenore reached out and laid her hand on his shoulder. "Just keep walking, Tigger."

It was her nickname for him when she was trying to be supportive.

"Okay, Eeyore," he whispered.

The climb up the hill was beginning to tire him. He felt the cramps in his abdomen growing worse and his legs were starting to really burn. If Lenore was in distress, she wasn't showing it. He hadn't noticed when she had drawn the revolver, but it was in her hand now. They didn't have that many bullets left. Ken had wasted so many of them on that one lone zombie. He felt like an idiot all over again.

"I'm glad Grandma isn't here," Lenore said at last.

"Me, too."

The older woman would have never made it at this pace and they would have had to leave her behind. No, Ken thought sadly, they would have had to kill her so she wouldn't have been eaten alive.

The top of the hill grew closer and he tried to set markers in his mind. He just had to make it to the next oak tree. To the next clump of wildflowers. To the next utility pole.

Lenore glanced at their pursuers again. Shaking her head, she struggled to increase their walking speed. Ken realized they had been slowing down as they walked uphill. The zombies didn't feel pain or discomfort. They were not going to slow down or get tired.

Glancing over his shoulder, he saw that the mob was gaining on them. They had probably closed the gap only by a few yards, but they suddenly seemed a lot closer.

"Keep walking. Those people should be here soon," Lenore urged.

As they crested the top of the hill, Ken saw the road had a long curve down into a valley. The area was heavily forested with oak and cedar trees. A few houses were tucked near the top of the flanking hills.

Starting downward, their momentum picked up. Ken felt relief until he realized that the zombies would also increase in pace. Shifting Cher's carrier to his other hand, he took several deep breaths. With the zombies yet to reach the top of the hill, the air was a lot cleaner.

"Lenore, if…" His voice caught in his throat.

"Don't say it," Lenore said gruffly.

"If they reach us first, please…"

"Don't say it!"

"After you kill me, please let Cher out of her carrier. Maybe she can make it out here. Maybe she can hunt or…" Tears began to choke him.

"Shut up!" Lenore shouted at him. "You're not going to die out here, you stupid asshole. I'll never let you die! As long as you are with me, they will never get you! Do you fuckin' understand me?"

Gazing into her dark flashing eyes, Ken believed her. Her vow was his lifeline. Grabbing onto it emotionally, he felt hope begin to drive away his fear. They were together. They had survived so much. Help was on the way. Together they would survive.

Lenore must have seen the new resolve in his eyes for she gave him a rare smile. "Stupid faggot."

"Hag bitch," he answered and grinned.

The zombie was upon them before he registered its presence. Hurtling out of the trees, it was a blur of screaming bloody flesh. Lenore fired, the shot echoing through the valley. The bullet hit the creature in the shoulder, flipping it around. It regained its balance and charged again, closing the gap between it and the living. Lenore took a breath, steadied her grip and fired just as it was about to sink its teeth into her outstretched hand. The bullet punched through its skull and it fell. Lenore jumped out of its way and the body crashed at her feet.

The second zombie emerged from the trees just as its companion fell. A woman; her skirt was a frayed bloody mess around chewed-up legs. It wasn't as fast as the first one, but she surged toward Lenore and Ken.

Lenore fired.

The zombie collapsed just as another zombie appeared behind her. Then another.

"Keep walking!" Lenore ordered Ken, firing at the zombies.

His grip tight on the carrier handle and the crowbar, Ken obeyed, understanding that she was right.

Lenore took down the zombies, then ran after him to catch up. Huffing, she struggled to reload the revolver.

"Six left," she muttered.

Ken glanced over his shoulder. The zombie parade was over the top of the hill and had gained on them. The dead were upwind, so Ken could barely smell them over the reek of gunpowder.

Cher was quiet now and he took a quick peek at her. She was cowering in the corner of her carrier, growling softly, afraid of the gunshots.

"You blew those assholes away," Ken said proudly to Lenore. He tucked the crowbar under his arm and shifted Cher to his other hand.

"I don't fuck around," Lenore replied as she finished reloading the gun.

Hurrying, trying to put more distance between them and the horde behind them, Ken and Lenore held hands.

24.
Salvation

Lenore's heart was beating so fast it hurt. She was trying not to show Ken her stark fear. The poor guy had looked ready to shit himself more than once already. Every muscle in her body was aching and she was developing a serious cramp in her side. Each step she took was painful now. Her hand and arm were in serious pain from the shots she had fired. The kick hadn't been that bad, but she had tensed too much.

She didn't want to look behind her, but she couldn't help herself. The zombies were closing in faster than she thought they would. They were probably fifty yards behind them now. Time was running out, but she refused to believe that their lives would end on this road.

Ken's hand was damp, but she didn't want to let it go. Knowing he was with her was comforting even if he was a big ol' wimp. If she was going to die today, at least it was with someone she genuinely loved. He was the biggest pain in her ample ass, but he was a loyal friend.

"Shit, shit, shit!" Ken exclaimed.

Returning her gaze to the road ahead, Lenore saw two cars mangled together in a terrible wreck at the sharpest point in the curve. One of the vehicles was a burned out shell. It was hard to tell when the accident had happened. The victims could have burned in the wreckage, or maybe they were the ones who had attacked. The world was so fucked up it was hard to say.

"Just keep calm and keep moving," Lenore instructed in a rough voice.

Ken let go of her hand and shifted the carrier from one hand to the other before gripping the crowbar. "Lenore, zombies…"

From around the smashed SUV a small cluster of zombies stepped into view. Their bodies were broken and terribly mutilated. Two appeared to have burned in the car. They were blackened husks.

Lenore's heart sped up while her lungs were strangled by vice grips as she raised the revolver. Setting her feet apart, she stopped and took aim. She had six bullets and five zombies.

The first shot missed them all. Sweat and tears blurred her vision and she blinked her eyes rapidly to clear her sight. She couldn't think about the zombies behind her gaining as she stood and fired at the ones before her. The next shot sent a zombie to the ground, but it slowly climbed to its feet. Beginning to panic, she tried to aim more accurately, but it only allowed the zombies to stumble closer. Pulling the trigger, she felt her arm go numb. Another zombie fell and stayed down. She fired until the gun clicked empty.

Three zombies were still advancing on them as a fourth crawled.

"I'm not dying today," Lenore said through gritted teeth and yanked the crowbar out of Ken's hands.

She charged. Halfway to the zombies, she felt her adrenaline hit. The world around her slowed as her vision became crystal clear. She swung the crowbar as hard as she could at the head of the first zombie. The impact traveled all the way up her arm, stunning her with its power, but then the zombie was falling, teeth shattered. Her next swing caught the zombie across the temple, sending it to its knees. She struck it again, the skull splintering as it crashed to the ground. The third zombie grabbed her hoodie, its teeth blackened and terrifying. She shoved the crowbar up through its neck and felt bone and muscles give way. Letting go of the weapon, the creature fell at her feet. Lenore yanked the crowbar out of its head.

Ken was shrieking, but she couldn't pay attention to him just yet. Slamming the metal bar down on the zombie heads, she felt their skulls shattering and their brains mashing into nothing. Twisting around, she saw the horde was much closer.

Terrifyingly, Ken was holding off a zombie using the cat carrier as a shield. Cher hissed furiously.

Lenore ran up behind the zombie and rammed the end of the crowbar into its skull. Yanking the crowbar out of the thing's head, Lenore shoved the zombie over with her other arm. Grabbing Ken's hand, they ran.

Her lungs were on fire and her legs felt like lead, but Lenore broke into a sprint. The stich in her side was even worse now and she fought the pain. Her ragged breath mingled with Ken's.

"Where's the gun?" Ken shouted.

Lenore didn't know. At some point she must have dropped it. She couldn't remember.

"Just run," she rasped.

The sound of the crowd of zombies tore at her nerves. She wanted to scream, she wanted to cry, but all she did was run.

"No, no, no," Ken sobbed as three zombies stepped out into the road. They were fairly intact, one woman with long blond hair, and two men. The blood on their bodies and faces looked very fresh. The bald man howled and broke into a run.

Shoving Ken behind her, Lenore brought the crowbar up, ready to fight.

"Try it, fucker!" she screamed.

A bus roared around the curve. Lenore barely registered it before it had barreled into the three zombies. The undead were pitched over the side of the road and into the trees like broken dolls.

The door opened. A woman with black hair wearing a red sweater jumped out. "Hurry!"

Lenore dropped the crowbar and ran. Ken's footsteps were a reassuring sound behind her. Leaping into the short bus, Lenore saw a female driver with lots of frizzy red hair staring out the windshield at the zombie crowd.

"Move to the back," a big white guy with a pleasant round face ordered.

Stumbling a little, Lenore dragged herself along the seats. A very cute black guy wearing a tracksuit and pristine white trainers grinned at her as he hopped over the rows on his way to the front. Falling into a seat, Lenore gasped in a deep breath of fresh air. Of course, Ken sat right next to her even though the bus was nearly empty. He set Cher on his lap and hugged the carrier close.

"Ed, what do we do?" the woman in the red sweater shouted.

Lenore could see that the crowd was nearly upon them. A scrawny older white guy with a hunting jacket on followed the black man out of the bus.

"Kill 'em, Jenni," Ed answered. "Can't have them heading to the fort."

The big round guy and the redheaded woman both grabbed their weapons and exited the bus.

"Why can't we just go?" Ken wailed.

Their rescuers opened fire. The sound of gunshots sent Cher into another hissing fit as Lenore flinched. She watched through the bus window as the group systematically killed the zombies that had been pursuing them. Their shots were clean and on target. Each bullet ripped through the heads of the undead, gore and blood spouting up into the air before the creatures collapsed. Soon the zombies lay in heaps all over the road. The rescuers walked carefully among them, making sure that each one was dead. At last, satisfied, they returned to the bus.

The first one onto the bus was the pretty girl with the black hair. Her checks were flushed with excitement and her eyes were sparkling. Her grin was almost disturbing in its glee.

"We took care of those fuckers," the woman said.

The rest of the crew climbed on board. The driver with the red hair shut the door and slowly pulled the bus around.

"We can't thank you enough," Ken exclaimed. "Oh my God! I thought we were goners!"

"Thank you for getting us," Lenore said, trying to breathe normally again.

The red sweater woman slid into the seat in front of them and reached out to grip each of their hands for a second. "I'm so glad we found you in time. I'm Jenni, with an *i*. I'm so happy to meet you."

"I'm Ken and this is my bestest girlfriend in the whole wide world, Lenore." Ken slung his arm around Lenore's shoulders and she harrumphed at him.

"Hi, Lenore and Ken. I have my own bestest friend in the whole wide world back at home. Her name is Katie." Jenni's face softened at the mention of her friend and her smile grew sweeter. "I know how important best friends are. Anyway, here in the bus that's Ed, Bill, Felix, and Katarina. We're from the fort in Ashley Oaks."

"A real fort?" Lenore asked, raising her eyebrows.

"We call it that, but it's really just a construction site that we built a wall around. But its home," Jenni said, shrugging. "And it's your home now, too." She peered into the carrier at Cher and let the cat sniff at her fingers.

Lenore unexpectedly felt tears in eyes at the thought of being safe again. She turned her head and stared out the window at the trees streaming past. Ken snuggled into her side, grinning impishly. It was good to see him acting and looking normal, but she wasn't about to tell him that.

"Girl, you were like Wonder Woman out there," Ken said to Lenore. "Jenni with an *i*, you should have totally seen her smacking the hell out of zombies with a crowbar. She was like Xena on their asses."

Jenni grinned. "Really? That's fucking awesome! I have an ax that I like to use sometimes. We need zombie killers. Those fuckers keep showing up. "

"I ain't using no damn crowbar no more. Or a gun," Lenore grumbled. She embraced her surliness, letting it fill her up. It felt good.

Felix, the handsome black guy, grinned at her. "So what are you going to use then?"

"Got a hunting bow? Or a crossbow?" Lenore asked. "Cause I got awards at church camp for archery."

"I think we can find you something," the big man named Bill assured her.

"That'll suit me just fine," Lenore decided.

As the bus sped down the country road toward their new home, Lenore deepened her scowl as inwardly she felt herself relax. Ken's fingers wrapped around her hand, and she flicked her gaze toward him.

"You were right," Ken said, smiling his wide, annoying smile. "We made it."

"You ain't never gonna die on my watch, asshole," Lenore promised him.

"You love me," Ken said, touched.

Lenore rolled her eyes. "You're family. I don't leave family behind."

Jenni smiled sweetly at her, her dark eyes sparkling. "Then you're going to fit in just fine at the fort."

To her surprise and Ken's, Lenore smiled back at Jenni.

The bus rolled past the "Welcome to Ashley Oaks" sign and toward the fort. Soaring above the trees, a water tower rose against the morning sky.

"Hey," Jenni said, pointing to what looked like a makeshift tent made out of blue tarp. "Does it look like someone is up there?"

"Going to rescue someone else?" Ken asked, peering up at the looming tower.

Jenni reloaded her weapons as the bus pulled up alongside the trees lining the area around the tower. Zombies were gathered at the base of the ladder that led upward.

"It's what we do," Jenni answered with a wink.

Bill and Felix helped Jenni up through a hatch in the roof as a figure appeared on the walkway of the water tower above.

Ken laid his head on Lenore's shoulder and she rested her cheek against his hair.

"We made it," Ken whispered.

Lenore nodded solemnly as she watched the rescue of two more people. She knew that the morning had been filled with miracles and she was grateful. Maybe Grandma was right when she said God opened doors when you least expected it. She was probably up in heaven right now smiling down at them. Maybe it was even her prayers that had brought them this far.

When the bus finally arrived at the fort, Lenore watched the terribly-thin rescued couple and their little dog disembark together. It could have gone so much worse than it had for her and Ken. She was grateful to finally be safe. Stepping out into her new home, she raised her eyes to the tall hotel rising above the fort.

"We'll be taking that over soon," a voice said near her.

Turning, Lenore saw a handsome white man with curly dark hair smiling at them. "My name is Travis. Welcome to the fort."

Lenore reached out to shake his hand, but a surge of emotion overwhelmed her and instead she threw her arms around him. "Thank you."

Travis held her close, like a father or a brother would, and said, "You're home now, hon."

Weeping, Lenore knew it was true. Ken rested his head on her shoulder and snuggled into her. They had made it at last. After all the loss and all the pain, they were safe. And she would fight for her new family and home until the day she died.

Epilogue

The truck slowly drew up to the RV, the engine hot and growling beneath the hood. Tito slid out of the driver's side door, shotgun at the ready. The RV's sides were smeared in blood and gore and the door was listing open.

"Ken? Lenore? Grandma?" he called out, though he knew it was futile.

A moan called out from inside the RV.

Tito watched the empty doorway warily, fearing what he would see. A zombie stumbled to the door, peering out at him. Its gnarled form was not familiar. It was not one of his friends.

Tito fired.

The zombie's head snapped back and it fell out of sight.

"Tito?" his wife's worried voice called out.

"Gimme a sec," he answered.

Esmeralda sat in the front seat holding onto their youngest. His older boy sat in the backseat holding a second shotgun.

Tito swiftly moved into the RV, sweeping his gaze over the interior. No other zombies emerged from the corners of the small living space. He quickly searched for any sign of his friends. If they had died inside, he would deliver them from their undead state. If they were mere corpses, he would burn them out of respect. Though all their clothes remained, there was no sign of his three friends. He considered going to check their campsite, but he knew it was fruitless. They would have only fled if zombies had invaded.

Stepping into the sunlight, he studied the surrounding area. Nothing stirred in the shadows of the trees.

"Are they there?" Esmeralda called out.

"No, baby," Tito said with a sigh. "They're not."

Swinging back into the truck, he slammed his door shut. Setting the shotgun next to him, he looked into his wife's dark eyes.

"You can't feel guilty," she said in a tender voice.

"I promised them I'd come back," Tito answered. His wife knew him too well. Guilt was eating him up.

"You did your best for them and for us," she reminded him.

He looked into the eyes of his children and knew she was right. "I just wish…" Shrugging, he drove onto the road. "We got a long way to go if we want to make it to Marfa by tomorrow morning."

"Daddy, is Grandpa going to be in Marfa?" Carlitos asked from the back seat.

"Along with a whole lot of other people. We'll be safe there," Tito answered, shifting gears. "There is nothing out here for us anymore."

The truck sped down the road, away from the RV, away from the Hill Country.

And the little town with a fort hidden in its heart.

Rhiannon Frater is the award-winning author of the *As the World Dies* trilogy *(The First Days, Fighting to Survive, Siege,)* and the author of three other books: the vampire novels *Pretty When She Dies* and *The Tale of the Vampire Bride* and the young-adult zombie novel *The Living Dead Boy and the Zombie Hunters.* Inspired to independently produce her work from the urging of her fans, she published *The First Days* in late 2008 and quickly gathered a cult following. She won the Dead Letter Award back-to-back for both *The First Days* and *Fighting to Survive,* the former of which the Harrisburg Book Examiner called 'one of the best zombie books of the decade.' Tor is reissuing all three *As the World Dies* novels. You may contact her by sending an email to rhiannonfrater@gmail.com or visit her online at rhiannonfrater.com. You can find out more about the *As the World Dies* trilogy and world by visiting astheworlddies.com.

–Author photo courtesy of Mary Milton

Printed in Great Britain
by Amazon.co.uk, Ltd.,
Marston Gate.